Re[illegible]
Suki Fleet

Innocence

"In the best possible way, Suki Fleet has a vise-like grip on my heart… the story is rich and powerful and ultimately hopeful."

—Boys in Our Books

"…readers looking for an emotional journey in an alternative tale will find it here."

—Library Journal

"It was wonderfully written and the emotion was there, I also enjoyed the story…"

—MM Good Book Reviews

Skeleton

"…the author did a beautiful job of creating a set of imperfect characters that work perfectly together. The story is engaging and tinged with suspense."

—Prism Book Alliance

"Such a lovely story and told in a way that captures the emotions beautifully. The characters are wonderful…"

—Because Two Men Are Better Than One

By Suki Fleet

Falling
Innocence
Skeleton

Published by Harmony Ink Press
LOVE STORY UNIVERSE
This Is Not a Love Story
Wild Summer

Published by Dreamspinner Press
http://www.dreamspinnerpress.com

FALLING

SUKI FLEET

DREAMSPINNER PRESS

Published by
DREAMSPINNER PRESS

5032 Capital Circle SW, Suite 2, PMB# 279, Tallahassee, FL 32305-7886 USA
http://www.dreamspinnerpress.com/

ISBN: 978-1-63476-154-3
Digital ISBN: 978-1-63216-985-3
Library of Congress Control Number: 2015904666
First Edition June 2015

Printed in the United States of America
∞
This paper meets the requirements of
ANSI/NISO Z39.48-1992 (Permanence of Paper).

Chapter 1

"JOSH!"

I stick my head around the stockroom door and just manage to duck in time as Soren flings a heavy black shoe at me. It hits the door and lands at my feet.

Even from across the shop floor I can see his sleek pierced eyebrow raised in challenge. "Can you see if there are any size nines in there while you're *hiding out* in the stockroom?"

I narrow my eyes. I am *not* hiding out.

Soren's just pissed because I left him to cope on the shop floor alone for the past half hour while I tried—and failed miserably—to deal with a small problem I have back at home.

I know I only half explained it to him but, damn it, it's *complicated.*

Sighing, I pick up the brogue and scan the shelves for a nine. There's one box left, tucked snugly next to the ceiling. Out on the shop floor, the phone next to the cash register is ringing. I decide it can wait and head toward the kitchenette to get the ladder. The shop is long and narrow, and the kitchenette is at the very back—a broom cupboard with a small sink and a kettle, though both are inaccessible with the ladder in the way.

"Josh! Phone!"

Rolling my eyes, I abandon my quest for the ladder and march back to the stockroom. I shove open the heavy door that separates the stockroom from the shop.

I'm only being his bitch because I feel guilty for abandoning him. And unfortunately he knows I feel guilty.

Soren is now crouched on the floor, measuring some tall kid's foot with enough concentration, you'd think he was calculating its surface area. He brushes his caramel-colored hair out of his eyes as I walk past, and I know he is watching me. I just wish it were for any other reason than the fact that he's pissed off right now.

Taking a deep breath, I smile tightly and pick up the receiver from behind the counter.

"Minstrel Shoes, how may I help you?"

"Josh, you said… you said you were going to call me back." Angus's voice has an edge of desperation to it even though I only spoke to him a few minutes ago, and I did not explicitly say I was going to call him back.

Soren is going to kill me for taking personal calls on the shop floor, but I guess Angus called me on this number because I switched my mobile off.

"We close at five thirty today," I improvise.

"*What*? Please, Josh, please! I need you to talk to Mum."

"Angus, I'm at work!" I hiss, trying to shield my mouth with my hand.

"She says… she says she needs something for self-defense…."

Knives.

I sigh heavily. Angus usually copes fine until Eleanor gets out the knives.

He makes a strangled noise that sounds almost like a sob, and I realize me being all annoyed with a stressed and decidedly unworldly eighteen-year-old is not going to help at all, so with a groan, I give up.

"Put her on," I say, running my hand down my face.

Behind me, I can feel Soren's blue eyes burning holes in my polyester work shirt. I know I'm not dealing with this situation too well, but everything that has happened is not exactly my fault.

"Eleanor?"

The voice at the other end of the line hums softly in response.

"Eleanor, it's okay. You're safe. Everything is okay. Angus is there. He'll look after you, and I'll be back later. You've got to put the knives away. We won't let anyone hurt you, okay?"

Eleanor makes some sort of noncommittal *hmm* that might mean she's listening to me, or it might mean she's coming up with other ideas about what weapons she can use in self-defense.

"You promise you're going to come back and take care of everything?" she whispers eventually.

I close my eyes.

"I promise," I say gently, meaning it as much as I can. I'm just not sure what the *everything* is that she wants me to take care of.

I tell her I'm going to finish up as soon as I can—which isn't really a lie. There's just no way I can leave early. Then I gingerly put the phone down and escape back to the stockroom before Soren can say a word. I retrieve the ladder from the kitchenette, get Soren's size nine brogues down, and make myself the epitome of helpfulness on the shop floor for the last hour before we close. Admittedly we only have another two or three people wander into the tiny old-fashioned shoe shop during this time, but I do all the annoying overfriendly crap we have training videos about, and that must count.

"JOSH." SOREN grabs my arm to stop me escaping as soon as it's five thirty. It's as though he has a sixth sense. "You've got to deal with this—" He gestures as if he can't quite think of the right words. "—*problem* outside of work hours."

We're the only two closing up, so running for the door and leaving him to lock up by himself wouldn't really have been fair.

I lock the back door and hand him the bunch of keys.

Soren flicks off the lights.

"Unfortunately, life doesn't just stop and wait until it's convenient," I say, watching the motion sensor in the corner of the shop flickering in the dark. I'm tired, weary.

"I fail to see why your neighbor being burgled is stressing you out so much."

"Eleanor has been like a mother to me since I moved into that flat and Angus is really just a kid. What am I supposed to do? Leave them to it?"

Soren sighs, flicking his lip ring with his tongue. I wish he wouldn't do that. It's incredibly distracting.

I run my hand through my hair and try to guide my thoughts away from that dangerous path. Soren is over the other side of the damn fence and off-limits in more ways than one.

Technically he's my boss, and despite being a dick sometimes, he's okay. It helps that he's completely, distractingly crushable, and that I've probably got enough shit on him and his weed habit that if there were any trouble between us, he would never dare make anything official. I'd never bring that up, though. I'm not like that. I mean, I'd hate for there to be any bad feeling between us. We're sort of almost friends. I think. Though I can't remember exactly what it's like to have friends anymore.

We exit the front of the shop, and together we pull down the heavy metal shutter and lock it to the floor.

"It never occurred to you that this isn't your problem?" he says, looking at me steadily as he unfolds his long limbs and stands back up.

"What? How can I walk away from her with a clear conscience when she needs me? Could you?"

"I mean," he says cautiously, "from what I heard you saying on the phone, she doesn't sound very mentally stable. Don't you think someone more qualified than you should check her out?"

I sigh. This is not a conversation I want to be having, especially not with Soren, whose opinions are always very black-and-white.

"She's not going to hurt anyone."

He raises his eyebrow, looks at me quizzically, and puts his hand on the metal shutter, shaking it to make sure it's locked securely. The sound echoes on and on down the empty walkways of the shopping center.

"So what's the deal with her son?"

Mentally I grit my teeth. We've been over this. Well, we've been over the fact that I have no intention of telling him about Angus. Unfortunately I think my reluctance to talk has piqued Soren's interest.

"He's eighteen, okay. A kid. Eleanor suffers from anxiety, and she's been too scared to go outside her front door for a long, long time. That alone freaks him out. But since last week, when she was robbed and threatened at knifepoint in her own home, she's been in this permanent state of panic. He doesn't know how to deal with any of it."

"And you do?"

I frown. "I just… I need to be there for her."

"Well, try and sort something out. I'm not getting paid enough to do your job as well as mine," he says bluntly, pulling a fat joint out of his cigarette packet. He lights up as we part ways.

I sigh. *If only it were that fucking easy, Soren.* If only.

"Josh." I turn as he calls my name and instinctively catch the small, light object he throws. "Chill out, yeah?"

A little shocked, I stare at the joint in my hand. Is he trying to get me arrested? I wonder if I should just bin it. I've smoked weed before, a long time ago, but only at other people's houses and using other people's weed, never on my own. Personal use, though, right? It's just one tiny (quite fat, actually) joint.

I don't move until Soren has vanished into the now dimly lit, empty shopping center. Aren't there security cameras everywhere watching us? I bet some fucking security guard is rubbing his hands together up in his snug little office. Maybe he has a little file with all our tiny indiscretions noted down so that one day he can blackmail us with them.

Fuck. Is this paranoia?

Maybe it's not just Eleanor who's been sent spiraling by all this. I close my fingers around the joint and head out of the shopping center.

ONE OF the weirdest things about working in a shop tucked away on the lower floor of a shopping center is that in winter you don't see any hint of daylight at all. It was dark when I got here at eight fifteen this morning, and it's dark now that I'm leaving at five forty-five too. My life is just one endless night.

It's not raining, but it has been because the streets glisten wetly in the lamplight. All along the High Street, garish Christmas lights sparkle too brightly, their vibrant colors blinking on and off with headache-inducing irregularity. I close my eyes for a moment, feeling tired and old. I'm not normally so gloomy, but maybe I've been possessed by the ghost of Christmas past or something. I shouldn't feel like this at twenty-five. I just want to get home to bed and shut it all out. I know that's not going to happen. I've got to make sure Eleanor is okay before I can shut the world out.... I made a promise.

The car park is dark and empty, but my falling-apart car sits faithfully where I left her. She's nothing special to look at, and is probably twice as old and ten times as rusty as most of the other cars that usually fill this car park, but it's more what she means to me and my sanity that makes her so important—she is my freedom, my get-out clause. She feeds that secret thought at the back of my mind of just being able to start her engine and drive away, never looking back.

"JOSH? JOSH? Is that you?"

Eleanor's panicky whisper greets me as I close the front door to her flat quietly behind me and step into the narrow hallway.

Of course it's me, I think. As far as I know, I'm the only one with a key apart from Angus… who should be here somewhere too.

"Yeah," I call, "it's me. I brought you both some fish and chips."

I hang my coat on one of the pegs in the hall, then walk into the kitchen.

"Angus is gone," she says dully, rocking back and forth as I lay the fish and chips on the table and glance around the cozily lit Victorian flat.

Although she seems a lot calmer now and there are no knives laid out anywhere that I can see, her face is blotchy as though she's been crying. I wonder if they have argued or disagreed about something, though I've never seen Angus angry, and I can't imagine even if he did get angry that it would be with Eleanor. He's too sweet with her.

"Want me to go look for him?" I ask.

After being at work all day, it's the last thing I want to do, but I know the guilt won't leave me alone if I don't at least offer.

She shakes her head, strands of soft, graying hair falling across her face.

She's barely forty, but she appears a lot older because she frowns and looks worried all the time. And more and more now, she hunches over as if she's trying to take up less space in the world. She's scared of her own shadow. But she wasn't always that way—the dark grip of anxiety has tightened its hold slowly, over time.

When I first moved into this block of flats five years ago, I could barely function. Eleanor took me firmly under her wing, showed me how to cook, how to shop for food (though she rarely went with me, even then), how to clean—how to cope. She showed me that someone cared. And that dying organ inside my chest came back to life a little bit.

Back then I didn't know she had a son she didn't see. Or an ex-husband with control issues. It surprises me (and it hurts too) because now Angus is here, I can see how much she adores him, and he adores her. But she told me she wasn't good for him back when he was small—I guess she means her anxiety. And I know leaving him with his dad was her choice, not something her husband forced her to do. Though, to be perfectly honest, what I've seen of Angus's father hasn't inspired any good feelings in me.

Since the beginning I've always seen Eleanor's anxiety as part of her personality. Some people are just more anxious than others, and their way of coping—or not coping—with the world is more pronounced, but her fears have escalated hugely since the burglary, and while that would be expected, I'm not sure her behavior is anywhere near normal anymore.

"He got upset and said he needed to go out. I'm scared he's had enough of me and is going back to his dad's." Her voice trembles over the words.

Today must have really got to him, then.

I put down the two plates I took out of the cabinet behind me and lay a hand on her arm. For the past couple of years, she's desperately wanted Angus to come and live with her. Even so, when he turned up on the doorstep two months ago and wanted to move in, it was completely unexpected and out of the blue.

"He won't do that," I say, only half convinced, because what goes through the mind of that kid, I can't even guess at most of the time. "He probably just needs a bit of space. You know how it is when you're eighteen." I shrug. I'm making it up. I was nothing like Angus at eighteen. Or rather, my life was nothing like Angus's life at eighteen.

Because eighteen is a black hole you can't remember, a little voice in my head whispers.

I try and encourage Eleanor to eat something, but she's too distracted. I'm starving though and inhale my dinner while she picks at her chips.

Ten minutes later the front door gently clicks open and then closed. Eleanor jumps out of her chair and disappears behind me making small anxious humming noises. I stand up. This sort of behavior puts you on edge however hard you try to remain calm.

For a moment Angus stands in the shadows of the hallway and looks at me the way he does sometimes, that expression I don't understand. Or maybe I do, and I just don't want to.

I can feel the relief rolling off Eleanor like great ocean waves.

"Angus," she whispers, as if she thinks perhaps he will disappear again if she says his name any louder.

"I just went for a walk," he says quietly, shaking rain out of his dark unruly hair—he has too much hair and the wildness of it makes me want to reach out and smooth it down. Sometimes the sunlight catches it and highlights it with gold, but mostly it looks as dark as the shadows he hides in.

He takes off his soaked cotton jacket and lays it carefully over the back of one of the dining chairs. I catch a flash of silver in the lining. Usually Angus wears black, as though there are no other colors. The silver is new.

"I'm glad you're here," he murmurs as he brushes past me.

Refusing to show how uncomfortable his words make me, I sit back down and try to act normally. I don't know why he gets to me like this. I wish he didn't.

It's a discomfort that built up over time.

He sits down opposite me, but he won't meet my gaze.

This is what unsettles me the most. Angus appears confident one moment, then crushingly shy the next. I have no idea how to deal with it, and so the ground is giving way beneath me.

"Grab a plate," I say airily as if I'm in control of the situation, and I start unwrapping the still warm portion of fish and chips I saved for him.

WE SIT and watch some inane program on the small portable television another neighbor kindly brought round after Eleanor's got smashed during the robbery, and then we help Eleanor to bed. It's early, but she has sleeping tablets that knock her out for a good twelve hours. I don't know how she'd cope if she had to get through the night without them. I don't know how *we'd* cope.

It's the fourth night we've done this, and I'm coming to dread the awkward moment when we close Eleanor's door. I mean, Angus is going to know I'm avoiding him if I say I'm going up to bed at seven o'clock every evening, isn't he? I should be able to deal with this, for fuck's sake. I'm twenty-five; he's eighteen. I should be able to say, "I'm going home now, good night," without feeling the need to explain further. But I do feel the need to explain because I *am* avoiding him. For some reason, I don't want him to know that.

We head back into the living room.

"I know I said I wasn't going to leave her on her own, but I just couldn't take it anymore," Angus says, sitting down at the dining table and concentrating on picking at the wax trail left by a candle.

I pull out a chair and sit down opposite.

"It's okay," I say, shrugging, because I have no idea what else I should say.

I've no idea if she's okay to leave on her own. I've no idea what could happen. Soren's words from earlier gnaw at me, and I wonder if he's right and calling a doctor would be the best thing to do. Last week, after the robbery, a nurse came out and gave Eleanor a prescription for sleeping tablets, but I don't think they realized the extent of her distress. At that point neither did Angus nor I.

It just seems so serious to involve anyone official—what if they decide she's not fit to be at home? The thought causes my chest to tighten. Old fears, memories of hospital corridors, locked doors, expressionless doctors, and psychiatric assessments rise to the surface. I push them down and wonder instead what would happen to Angus. What would he do? Would he cope on his own? Would he end up going back to his controlling father? Questions I'm afraid of the answers to—and that's why I tell myself most of the time she's not that bad.

"You're probably sick of this. Us," Angus mumbles into the tabletop, bringing me out of my thoughts.

I roll my eyes. I realize this situation is better than the usual one of Angus's coming on to me and my pathetic attempt to ignore it like it's not happening, but I don't deal with people feeling sorry for themselves very well, so I try to change the subject.

"Fancy a smoke?"

I pull Soren's joint out of my pocket and lay it on the table between us.

I only ask because it seems like a quick-and-easy way for me to get out of here. We'll smoke, and it'll make both of us relaxed and a bit sleepy, and I can make my excuses to go. And to be honest, the stupid thing has been weighing me down since Soren threw it to me, and I'll be glad to get rid of it.

It's only when Angus meets my gaze for a fraction of a second that I think "fancy" was completely the worst word to use.

He nods. "Can't in here, though. Eleanor doesn't like smoking. She hates the smell."

Inwardly I groan. The rain is still whispering against the window, the world beyond fathomless and black. There's no way we're going to be smoking outside tonight. I feel like I've unwittingly boxed myself into a corner.

"Come on, then," I say darkly, mentally assessing how tidy I left my flat this morning.

Angus looks far too happy about this.

What the hell am I doing?

"THIS IS a one-off, and I'm tired, so don't get all offended when I chuck you out," I say as we stand on the stairs. I keep one step above him to exaggerate my height even more. It makes me feel more like the grown-up if I treat him like a child. "I don't like visitors. Very few people have been up here. Feel privileged."

I mean it as a joke, but I don't smile.

My tiny flat is on the top floor. Its four rooms would have been the servants' quarters back when this house was built in the late nineteenth century. I'm secretly very proud of it, and when Angus follows me inside and goes "Whoa," some little place inside me lights up like a Christmas tree.

"I like books," I say nonchalantly, because it's a complete understatement. Because I am *obsessed.* Books, stories, poetry, words.

The walls that aren't lined with shelf upon shelf of them are papered with pages saved from obscurity: weird poems, outdated theories, stories. In fact, the whole flat wouldn't look out of place as the outlandish library in some eccentric stately home, the furniture all dark wood and plush velvety fabrics in eclectic colors.

Angus runs his fingers down the old fabric-covered spines of the books that line the shelves in the hallway. "Have you read all of them?"

I spin round, incredulous. "Are you joking?"

"Is that a no, then?"

He looks so uncertain. What does he think I do up here on my own?

It drives me a little crazy that this boy has to have everything so definite and sure. It makes me want to wrong-foot him and infuriate the certainty out of him.

But instead, he somehow infuriates the certainty out of *me*.

"Does that seem so unlikely?" I ask as I switch on the light in the kitchen and quickly switch it back off again, guiding Angus into the living room as it occurs to me all the explicit sex scenes I papered on the kitchen walls are not what I want Angus to see right now. Kitchen sex seemed like a wonderfully perverse idea when I decorated, but I don't want to put any more ideas into Angus's probably already overstimulated imagination.

Faintly he whispers something.

I'm not sure if it's in answer to my question or not. The living room seems to have captured his attention somewhat.

"You don't have a TV," he says more loudly, spinning round and looking a little mesmerized. "And you've got clouds on your ceiling."

I allow myself a grin. "Technically, they're not clouds."

I flick the switch on the wall behind him, turning on the overhead light so he can see a little more clearly.

"Nebula," he says, meeting my gaze with strange intensity.

The room is still pretty shadowy, and usually I love the warm low lighting, but right now I wish it were brighter.

"How? Is it wallpaper?"

I give in. "They're just photographs from the Internet that I had blown up."

"But it's so seamless," he says, turning round. "Is it accurate?"

"Pretty much. Bit of research, and voilà, the universe. No TV, remember." I try to smile, but it's a bit of a painful memory. I did the ceiling before I did the walls, back when I wasn't really coping.

"It's amazing."

This kid who doesn't smile too often is grinning widely, and all at once I'm glad I brought him up here. It's not often I feel like this either.

But all the good he does with one sentence, he destroys with the next.

"Why do you never invite anyone back here?"

"Why do none of your friends from school visit?" I retort helplessly.

He wasn't to know, but his question hit a nerve, and it seems from the stunned expression on his face, mine did too. Right into the heart of things.

I close my eyes.

Up here under the eaves, the rain sounds heavier, and I'm so tired, I feel as though I want to curl up in my warm bed and let it lull me to sleep, but instead I slump down into the armchair behind me, hugging my knees to my chest and thinking how strange it is having someone here. How strange it is watching Angus's broad-shouldered silhouette as he stands looking out my window at the brightness that lights up distant London.

It's strange, but I'm surprised to find I don't mind, not really. Even if we don't really know what to say to each other now.

When Angus first moved in a couple of months ago, he was lonely, and Eleanor asked me if I would make him feel welcome. So I tried, and we got on pretty well for a few weeks, but then he found out I was gay and things started to get all weird between us. Well, it was either that or the fact that I chased his dad away one day when he was hammering on the door and trying to be all intimidating. Perhaps Angus now sees me as some sort of knight in shining armor.

It makes me want to laugh at how wrong he is.

I pick up the matches off the mantelpiece—it's a shame I can't be bothered to fetch any wood to light a fire—and sink back down into the chair as I light the joint.

"Hey," I say softly. It's the closest he'll get to a peace offering.

His shoulders tense, and he turns around, his expression telling me how unsure he is. Of me… of being here. He's just a kid, I tell myself. A kid who's as lonely as I am.

I take a drag and pass him the joint. "Sit down. Want a drink?" I offer recklessly.

"Of what?" he asks, leaning back awkwardly on the threadbare velveteen sofa and trying not to cough as he takes too greedy a hit.

His inexperience is a turn-on. It probably shouldn't be. No. It *definitely* shouldn't be.

"Beer. It's not particularly strong. I don't want to get you drunk," I add before I can stop myself. The guilt I'm feeling for upsetting him just now is doing strange things to me—things like causing this weirdly protective urge to look after him.

He nods, and I leave him staring around the room as I retrieve a couple of glasses and the beer from the kitchen.

This is the last thing I thought I would be doing this evening. To be perfectly honest, playing host to a lonely eighteen-year-old is up there with firing rockets at the moon.

I FORGOT how weed makes your mind elastic and alcohol cuts your mind's ties with your tongue. It's been years since I've felt like this, drunk this much with anyone else around. And though it feels kind of nice, I wish I could shut up.

We're lying on the sofa on the verge of slipping off—there is not enough room. I can't remember how we ended up here in the first place. I think I must have fallen over it on the way back from the kitchen with the third or fourth round of drinks. Angus is gripping my arm to stop me sliding, and I'm laughing so hard it hurts. God, happiness is painful.

In between my laughter, I'm telling him in all seriousness about what makes up the darkness of the Horsehead Nebula. It seems crucial that I impart this information to him, but for some reason he snickers every time I say *horsehead*, and in a rush of giddy laughter, we land in a heap on the floor, knocking bottles and glasses flying.

We stop laughing at exactly the same moment, and though the pleasure of it still rolls through me, it's now mixed with a different, deeper sort of bliss.

A bliss that comes from having another body lying close to mine, so warm and strong, another heart thumping excitedly.

It's been so long since I've been so warmly tangled with someone. I didn't realize quite how much I've missed it.

I stroke my fingers down a fabric-covered limb because, I tell myself, it's hard to know where I end and he begins. I'm just curious, I tell myself. It's not because I like the weight of his slightly stockier form pressing me into the floor, or the steady warmth that has suddenly surrounded me.

His head is on my chest. I think I can feel the pulse of him against me somewhere low down. My own pulse is like the electricity of a thundering machine, rushing blood and longing round my pathetic, lonely body.

I wish this didn't feel so good, so right. I wish it wasn't making me hard. I should push him off. I should open the window and drink in lungfuls of cold London air to cure this madness.

But I don't.

We shift like a moveable sea, as a single being. When I feel the heat of Angus's breath on the side of my neck and his fingers, somehow in this mess of limbs, find mine, I turn my head toward his and his mouth opens against my cheek and, sloppily, he kisses me.

Again I'm just curious. It's not because I want him so much as I just want *someone*.

He's not good at this, but what he lacks in experience, he makes up for with sweetness, as when he doesn't find my mouth the first time, he searches so tenderly, eyes squeezed shut tight until I relent and turn my head so our lips brush and we hungrily press our mouths together. Deliciously, he whimpers when I flick my tongue against his and grinds his erection into my thigh. He tastes so smoky, and his mouth is so hot and liquid, I want time to explore it. I want to get lost in the taste of him.

I kiss him deeply, and the sound he makes reverberates down my throat and awakens something so long dormant inside my chest, it aches.

Willing and eager, he lets me roll him over onto his back and pin his arms above his head. I'm not curious anymore. Alcohol has diminished my usually rigid self-control, and I know exactly what I want. I want him naked and trapped beneath me, pressed against the floor. Pushing my hips hard against his, I nuzzle his neck, drinking in the earthy scent of him while he tries to kiss any part of me he can reach. I am desperate with need, and in some still sober corner of my mind, I know that if I kiss his mouth again, this is going to go too far, too fast. Cautiously I lick and then suck the supple skin at the juncture of his neck and shoulder. He tilts his head to give me better access and moans encouragingly. I don't know where this desire to mark him has come from. It feels primeval. When I start nipping and rolling his skin between my teeth, he gasps and yelps, so lost to the sensation, I know this is going to make him come. He trusts me not to hurt him, and it's the biggest turn-on.

"Josh," he moans breathlessly.

And just like that, it's as though a bucket of icy water has been poured over my head.

Fuck, I don't even know why, but hearing my name has shattered whatever fragile spell was working its magic between us.

I recoil away from him, my hand covering my mouth, disgusted with myself.

I'm suddenly sober as all hell and horrified that I let things get this far with Eleanor's son. Eleanor's completely inexperienced and unworldly *eighteen*-year-old son. Eleanor, whom I owe far too much to. Eleanor, who trusts me. How did I let myself get so carried away?

And it's not just that—I don't do sex with people I know. I don't do intimacy. People don't whisper my name as if I am holding their heart in my hands. I can't deal with being so close to anyone. I feel sick.

I don't know what to do.

In my mind I'm rushing toward the bathroom, locking the door, and throwing up, but in reality my limbs feel like lead and I can't move. I crawl into the chair next to the sofa, wanting it to swallow me.

"Josh? What did I do wrong?" I hear him whisper.

He's not feeling sorry for himself this time. He's scared and he's hurt. He really thinks he *has* done something wrong. And I know from other things he's said it's probably because of that fucking shit of a father he feels like this—he doesn't think it's me who has a problem, he automatically thinks it's him.

I am a complete shit—I don't answer. The words just won't come. Even though he has done nothing wrong, nothing at all.

Shakily he gets up off the floor and sits on the edge of the sofa. He sets a few of the bottles upright. The gentle clinking as they touch one another is the only sound in the room. I expect him to leave. I want him to leave. *Go, just go*, I will him.

Although I spend most of my time on my own, I've never needed to *be* alone more than I do right now. I wish I could take this hour back.

"Josh?" he murmurs and brings his hands up to his face.

"You should go home, Angus," I say tightly.

Go home and never come back.

Chapter 2

NEXT MORNING I'm woken by a knock. It's quiet and not urgent but still I leap out of bed in case Eleanor needs me, in case it means something has happened downstairs. It's only when I pass the mess of glasses and bottles I didn't bother clearing up in the living room and catch the faint, stale smell of smoke in the air, that I recall what happened last night, and I hesitate before opening the door. Dread pools low in my stomach, and I squeeze my eyes shut.

Please don't be Angus.

Slowly I unlock the door, and when I open it, I frown.

It's not Angus.

It's not anyone.

In the bedroom, I can hear my 7:00 a.m. wake-up call going off. The hallway is empty, although there is a strong scent of coffee coming from somewhere. I look around, puzzled, and then on the floor at my feet, I see one of Eleanor's brightly colored round tin trays laden with coffee and croissants from the bakery down the road.

I just stare at it.

I don't know what to do.

The thought that he could have poisoned them flares briefly in my paranoid mind, but I quickly snuff it out. I know I'm being ridiculous. I just don't understand why he'd do this for me when I'm the one who messed up last night. I'm the one who should have had more self-control and not allowed it to happen. And this has to be from Angus. Eleanor hasn't left the house for so long.

Carefully picking up the tray, I close the door and take it through to the kitchen, where I put it on the table and sit unmoving in front of it until the coffee has gone cold.

I'M LATE for work. I spend half an hour sitting in my car in the car park, picking at the black tape that holds my CD player in place, and wondering what the hell I should do. I have the desire to start the car again and go, to drive and drive and drive until I'm poised over the edge of something and can go no farther. It's just a fantasy, but I need it.

I didn't even check in on Eleanor as I usually do in the morning. I just left. My self-loathing feels a lot like nausea today.

I can't stop thinking about how I kissed Angus. I can't stop thinking about the warmth of his body against mine, how close we were, and how that feeling turned so wrong when he said my name and brought me back to myself. I let him kiss me, knowing he likes me. I let him kiss me, knowing how young he is.

It was as though I'd been having a wet dream and it'd twisted into a fucking nightmare.

I *wanted* him. So badly.

No, I correct myself sternly, I wanted *someone*. He just happened to be there.

Perhaps I just need to get laid. Sex is just a physical need, after all.

SOREN IS sorting out the cash in the till with his maroon-and-gold tie wrapped around his head. He raises an eyebrow as I walk past.

"Someone's in a good mood this morning," he says.

"You look ridiculous," I say in response.

"Your face is ridiculous."

"Fuck you."

"You'll go far in the world of customer service."

"You're not a customer."

"No, but I get to fire you if you piss me off too much." He smiles like the Cheshire cat, and I narrow my eyes and glare.

I spend the morning cleaning things. Anything. I take all the shoes off the shelves one by one to clean away nonexistent specks of dust as though my life depends on doing such pointless tasks. I vacuum the stockroom until I manage to vacuum something I shouldn't, and the stupid thing makes a weird noise and stops vacuuming altogether.

Soren keeps out of my way, thank God.

I'm taking my brief lunch break, sitting on the stockroom floor, staring at my uneaten sandwich, when Soren pokes his head round the door.

"There's some boy on the phone for you."

I feel like throwing up.

"Tell him I'm not here."

"No fucking way," Soren says, raising his eyebrows as if I've asked him to go kick a kid in the stomach. Funnily enough *kicked* is exactly how my stomach feels right now. "I'm not doing your dirty work. Go talk to him yourself, and make it quick." Soren disappears back onto the shop floor.

Reluctantly I drag myself up.

Soren is with a customer but he watches me as I walk over to the counter and pick up the handset. The plastic is cold in my hand.

"Hello?" My voice is flat.

Silence.

I sigh. I should just put the phone down. But I don't.

"I don't know what to say to you," Angus says eventually in a voice so small and quiet I can barely hear him above the general rumble of shopping center noise going on around me. "Mum missed you this morning."

"Tell her I'll call in later."

"Okay," he says still in that small voice.

There is a pause, and then he hangs up.

I lean against the counter. The sharp corner digs into my stomach, but I don't move. I suddenly feel so ill, I think I need to lie down.

ALL AFTERNOON, the rain outside is torrential. Not that we'd know it in our cave of a shop if it weren't for all the drenched, complaining customers.

"Think you might be able to give me a lift to Bridge Street?" Soren asks, a mock-hopeful look on his face, as we close up.

"Yeah, okay." I give him my best put-upon face and sigh. Of course I don't really mind.

Bridge Street is where Soren's dealer lives. I've been there before, which is why I've got so much shit on him and his drug habit. It really must cost him a fortune. I secretly hope he wants me to wait around while he scores as that will take even longer.... Except then I would have a car full of drugs. Even so, I think I'd rather wait. Right now I would probably be willing to drive him the one and a half hours to Brighton to pick up a stick of rock if he asked me. Anywhere that isn't home.

The rain is still absolutely pouring down as we walk out of the shopping center. Rivers of glistening water run down the sides of the streets. We leap over them and then run, exhilarated and freezing, toward the car park.

It amuses me to watch Soren fold his long skinny limbs into my tiny car. I'm not short, but Soren looks like a spider shoved in a shot glass.

"Comfortable?" I ask.

"It's not exactly a limo, is it?" Soren says, knocking the gear stick as he shifts around and looks suitably apologetic as I scowl at him. "So, this is probably a bad idea considering the small space we're in, but how's your problem working out?"

"You'll be pleased to hear I'm fucking things up even more," I say heavily as I pull out onto the main street.

Soren looks horrified. "Why would you think I'd be pleased?"

Distracted, I have to swerve sharply away from the pavement. "I don't know," I mutter.

"I mean it, Josh. I know we, well, we don't know each other that well." Not for Soren's want of trying, I admit as I think back to all the times he's invited me out with his friends, or to his house, or to meet his girlfriend. "But I can see this stuff is really getting to you. I can see you're stressed out, and what I'm trying to say is, I know I can be a dick to you, but sometimes I'm just trying to cheer you up, and if you ever want to talk… I'm here."

I stare fixedly ahead as though I haven't heard him.

Why would I want to talk about it? Why on earth would I want an audience as I fuck up everything I do and land on my face?

"Um, Josh?" He touches my arm. "You know that turning you take for Bridge Street?" I grip the steering wheel. "Well, it was back there."

The wheels spin a little on the slick road surface as I swing the car round in the middle of the traffic and cause a chorus of angry beeps. Soren actually grips the handrail above his head.

As we turn into the street of Victorian two-up, terraced houses, I find it faintly amusing, in a painful sort of way, that Soren doesn't know what else to say to me. I've got my "fuck off and leave me alone" attitude down perfectly.

"Thanks for the ride. You can just drop me here if you like."

I think he just wants to get out of the car as quickly as he can. And as soon as I stop, he hops out, slams the car door, and sprints through the rain down the street to number twenty-eight.

He knocks, the door opens, and he vanishes inside.

Miserable little house after miserable little house, rubbish piling up in front of them, windows broken or boarded up. It's not my concern, but I hope Soren isn't getting in too deep. Do these people ever let you just walk away?

I keep the engine running and stare into the darkness.

Some kid is banging on the door of the house right next to the dealer's house now. Both hands, over and over, like he doesn't care how much it hurts his fists—like he's desperate. I don't think he gets that whoever lives there either isn't in or they don't want to answer the door. I don't think he gets that someone is going to come out of one of those other houses—out of the dealer's house maybe—and shut him up if he doesn't do it himself soon.

The narrow little street is wide enough for two cars at a push, but only if you don't mind clipping wing mirrors as you go, and I know I can't sit here in the middle of the road forever. It's just that the steady noise of the windscreen wipers as they drift back and forth and the low growl of the idling engine lull me and make me believe I can ignore that little worm of guilt that whispers I should get back and see how Eleanor is. Anything could have happened. None of this is her fault either.

I wish I could sit here forever.

Urgent tapping against my window snaps me out of my reverie, and I jump back in shock. A sharp face appears in the rain-streaked glass.

The kid who was banging on the door of the house is now knocking on my window. His hair is plastered to his head, and his soaking clothes stick to his skin. Up close he looks a little older than I thought—definitely not a kid.

"Open your window a sec!" he says, placing his palm against the glass. His expression is a little too desperate.

The black eye and the deep cut above his lip look fresh. This whole area is dodgy. Maybe he was looking for the dealers and got the wrong house. I don't want any trouble.

I glance round the car and realize I've not locked the doors.

So I do what seems like the most sensible option—put the car in gear and start to drive off.

I've gone barely a meter when an almighty yell stops me dead.

What the hell?

I glance in the wing mirror and see the boy doubled over, his face twisted up in agony.

It occurs to me that this could be a trick to get me out of the car, but my annoying conscience won't let me drive off, so I reverse back up and wind the window down.

"What the fuck were you doing? You just drove over my foot!" the boy spits, breathing heavily. He's bent over clutching his foot, obviously in pain.

"I didn't know you were stood so close to my car.... Can you walk on it?"

He yelps as he tries to put his foot on the ground, and something twists sickly inside me—I don't think he's putting it on. I get out and reluctantly help him round to the passenger side of the car. The horrible freezing rain soaks through my jacket in seconds. The least I can do is take him to the hospital, and if I've broken his foot, I doubt he's going to be much trouble.

Sitting in the passenger seat, he's shivering as though he's been out in this rainstorm for hours. I suspect his lips are blue, but in the dim car light, he just looks unearthly pale. I turn up the car heater to full blast, but it doesn't get much warmer.

"Do you normally go to such extreme lengths to get a lift?" I ask wryly, but he just wraps his arms around his body and folds forward, breathing as though he's run a great distance.

We drive to the hospital in deep silence.

"What are you doing?" he asks in a shocked voice as he looks up and sees I've stopped in an ambulance bay outside A & E.

"Taking you to hospital, where did you think we were going? Your foot might be broken."

"It's fine. My foot will be fine. Please just… take me somewhere else."

Now he doesn't look so old anymore. I'm guessing he's barely twenty, maybe younger, and I hate that I recognize that fear in his eyes, but I do. He looks haunted. I hate that it brings back old buried feelings of being so young and unable to see a way out.

"Okay… where do you live?" I ask, trying to remain detached.

"What?"

"Tell me where you live, and I'll take you home."

"Could you just drop me in town somewhere? I'll get home from there."

"You're freezing and soaked through and it's pissing it down out there. I ran you over, and I'm not just leaving you somewhere in the rain."

My guilt about running him over won't let me get away with dumping him somewhere and trying to forget about him.

For a few moments, he studies me, trying to work out if I mean what I say.

"Can we start over?" he asks softly, and despite the bruises and my better judgment, I nod.

"I'm Oskar," he says, holding out his hand and all at once coming to life.

"Josh."

His fingers are freezing.

"Hey," he says, sitting straighter. A pained expression flickers across his face, but his eyes are suddenly bright with a curious fire. "Did you think I was going to mug you or something? Is that why you drove off?"

"Do you trust everyone you meet?"

He looks at me quizzically. "Only fools trust *anyone*."

"You look too young to be so cynical. So if you weren't going to mug me, what did you want?"

"The time… and maybe a ride…." He squeezes his eyes shut.

However much I don't want to admit it, I can't stand to see anyone in pain, or hurting.

An image from last night fills my mind—of Angus's hurt expression as he wondered what the hell he'd done wrong. I try to shut it out. I wish I knew when I'd started to care so much about him, but it's something that has crept up on me, like a thief in the night.

"It's six fifteen and you've got a ride. So where do you want to go?" I say, trying to distract Oskar (and me) by continuing to talk.

He slips down in his seat and throws his head back. "Honestly… I don't know."

The lost way he says this makes me suspect he has *nowhere* to go, no home to return to, and it pushes me into offering something I wouldn't normally offer. And despite saying only fools trust anyone, right now he is in pain and vulnerable.

"Come back with me and let me give you a change of clothes, at least."

He considers this and then says quietly, "Okay."

Hugging his foot, he closes his eyes and curls up in the seat like a cat.

I PARK as close to the house as I can get. Oskar still can't put any weight on his foot, so I awkwardly slip my arm under his shoulders and half carry him inside. He barely weighs anything, although he is of a similar height to me, and I feel afraid to hold him too tightly lest I break him.

We pass Eleanor's front door and, gathering myself together, I stop. I can't avoid this moment forever.

"Wait here. I won't be long," I tell Oskar as I lean him against the wall and get Eleanor's keys out of my bag to unlock the door.

Oskar hops, wincing, to the stairs, where he slumps down, shivering again. He seems to alternately fire and fade. Any burst of energy leaves him exhausted. I find myself wondering when he last ate anything, and I mentally go through the contents of my fridge.

I slide the key into the lock—the familiarity of this task makes my heart ache—and I push the door open.

Inside, the flat is too quiet, and deep, awful dread seeps inside me, my rational thoughts replaced with formless anxiety. What if something terrible has happened because I wasn't here to stop it?

I flick the light on in the hall and hurry into the living room, every sense on high alert. A little lamp glows in the corner, illuminating the sofa and Angus's sleeping form curled beneath a blanket. Relief washes over me. As silently as I can, I make my way across the room. I've got to check on Eleanor. She's the one I *should* be most worried about.

"I gave Mum her tablets early and helped her to bed. She was so anxious, and I just couldn't take it anymore."

I spin round. Angus is sitting up, hugging the blanket tightly. His hair falls messily in front of his gray eyes. He looks exhausted.

"You don't have to do this, you know. It's not like you're *related* to us or anything. You don't owe us anything," he carries on tiredly, and for the first time, I detect a little bit of bitterness in his tone—the way he says *related* as if it's a curse. "When you didn't come, I told her you had some emergency at work or something. I said I wasn't completely sure. I didn't want to lie."

I know I should probably say something. Like apologize or say it's not true, I do owe her, and Eleanor has been my only family for so long. But the right words aren't coming, and "You didn't do anything wrong last night" comes out instead.

As I stare at him, it occurs to me how much he looks like her, like Eleanor. He has her leaf-shaped eyes, her straight nose, and her dimples when he smiles, and yet he is so much himself—so beautiful and so completely unaware of it….

I close my eyes. I need to stop this.

"I feel kind of… weird," I hear Oskar say faintly, stumbling through the doorway, looking confused and running his hands through his hair.

At the sound of another person's voice, Angus looks round and jumps in shock, pressing himself back against the sofa, stuttering, "Wh-who?"

Before I can answer and reassure him he is not about to be fucked over again (because, yeah, Angus got threatened in the robbery too, and it's just better somehow that I bury how I feel about that along with everything else), I notice that Oskar looks even paler than before, and I'm not sure how that's even possible. His movements are dizzily uncoordinated. Without warning, his arms drop, and his face goes slack. I reach him just as his knees give way and he swoons toward the floor.

"Angus!" I yell, but he's already there, lifting Oskar with me and helping carry him to the sofa.

Surprisingly Angus takes charge of the situation, checking he's still breathing (which thankfully he is) and telling me to raise Oskar's legs.

"Have you got something with a stopwatch on?" Angus asks me calmly.

Actually, I've never seen him so calm and together. I am at sea. Oskar looks dead, and the thought chills me to the very core.

"I…. Yeah, here." Shakily I pull out my phone.

"I need to check his pulse. Can you time me?"

I nod and fiddle around, unable to work out where on earth the stopwatch is.

"He's just passed out. He'll be okay," Angus says, watching me closely.

I pass him the phone and wish he wasn't seeing me like this, but being shaken up is not something I can hide.

I watch as Angus wraps the blanket around Oskar's unconscious body.

"He's really cold, and his clothes are soaking."

"I brought him back here to give him some dry clothes. I ran over his foot," I admit, feeling completely crap about everything.

Angus nods, counting. "We should take a look at his foot."

As we're taking off Oskar's worn-out shoe, I watch a little color come back into his skin and his eyelids flicker.

Even with his sock on, I can see his foot has swollen to twice the size it's supposed to be.

"I think it's probably broken. We should take him to the hospital," Angus says.

"All right. What about changing his clothes?"

Angus shakes his head. "He needs an X-ray."

"Now?"

Angus nods, biting his lip when he looks at me.

"Okay, help me carry him to the car," I say. I need to pull some control back. I need Angus to still see me as the one in charge, though I'm not sure why.

"What about Mum?" Angus asks worriedly as he grabs his coat and locks the front door.

"My car is only parked by the curb, it's not far. It'll only take two minutes."

Angus stops and looks down at the cracked tiles that decorate the floor. I can't see his face behind all that hair.

Perplexed, I stop too. And then I realize.

"I mean, it'd be easier if you came with me to the hospital to help me, but I can probably lift him on my own." I owe him far more than this simple concession. "But if you want to come, I'm sure she'll be okay. Those tablets knock her out completely."

"It's dark," he says quietly.

And I know he means *What happens if they come back in the middle of the night to finish the job, like Eleanor is so sure will happen, and we're not there—we're stuck at the hospital.*

"I'll make sure we're not gone for long. Trust me."

OSKAR IS still pretty out of it, and we strap him into the back seat as best we can.

Things don't seem quite so weird with Angus, so I ask, "How did you know to take his pulse and to raise his legs and all that stuff?"

Now I think about it, he's generally very calm with Eleanor too (apart from when she gets super anxious and starts getting the knives out). I guess that's why I thought he could cope being at home to look after her all day.

"Um…," he says as though he's talking to his hands.

I swallow, reluctantly admitting that despite the fact it drives me insane, I like his shyness quite a bit. It makes something inside me go weak with want.

"I did sport science at school. I was really into all that stuff."

I don't take my gaze off the road, but I'm hyperaware of every little movement he makes: brushing his hair out of his eyes, looking out the window, glancing at me.

"I wanted to be a physical therapist, but my dad laughed at me and told me all I'd ever be good for was stacking shelves in the supermarket. He said I needed to get real and get a job to pay for my food and rent. He refused to buy any of the course books I needed for the A-level subjects I took, so I couldn't keep up in class. That's why I didn't finish school."

Angus had never told me that before. He'd just said he had some time off school. His reaction to my comment about no school friends visiting makes a lot of sense now.

"Your father is a complete bastard, you know," I say, feeling an honest-to-God hatred for the man.

To my surprise Angus laughs.

"Sorry…." He blushes, though I've no idea why he is embarrassed. "I can just imagine you saying that to his face, though, and him going ballistic, and you standing there all stone-faced and intimidating like last time."

Me, intimidating? I have no idea where he gets these ideas about me from. All I did was tell the fucker to piss off or I'd call the police and get him arrested for harassment. It was hardly intimidating behavior, but at least he heeded my words and didn't come back.

And it was pretty unlike me, really. Confrontation of any sort, and I'm headed for the hills. Literally. I'm not trustworthy. Or loyal.

IT'S HALF eleven by the time we get back from the hospital. Things are beginning to grate on my nerves, and every time I look at the rough plaster cast around Oskar's foot and ankle, I feel the hole inside me getting bigger and I know I have to put something right. And not just with Oskar.

But I don't know how.

We used my name and details to sign Oskar in at the hospital. He pretended to be more out of it than he actually was so he didn't have to answer any awkward questions, which seemed to stem his panic about being there a little, though I know he still wasn't happy we'd taken him there. But I'm glad we did because his foot *is* broken.

As soon as we're back, Angus rushes inside to check on Eleanor, who is still sleeping the deep and soundless sleep of the drugged, and then helps me carry Oskar upstairs. All of a sudden he is inside my flat again. They both are.

"Make yourselves at home. I'll go sort us out some food." I wave my hands vaguely toward the living room and then vanish into the kitchen to try and deal with how I feel about this and to think about what I'm going to do. I can't chuck Oskar out with a broken foot—*especially when I broke it*—but I really don't like the thought of him staying here either. I don't know anything about him. And more than that, he's in my space. I need to be on my own. It's how I have learned to function.

I pull some noodles and various vegetables out of the fridge and stare blankly at them until some sort of autopilot takes over.

Cooking takes me away from thinking, and I become immersed in what I'm doing—chopping, stirring, adding a bit of spice, a bit of rice wine, looking for enough plates and glasses in the cupboard above the sink….

I don't realize Angus is standing in the doorway watching me until it's too late, and I inhale sharply and stumble against the cooker in shock.

"Um, Oskar's shaking pretty bad. Do you have some dry clothes he could wear?" he asks hesitantly, looking everywhere but at me.

Okay, so we're back to being weird, I think resignedly.

"Yeah, just stir this, and I'll go get some," I say, pointing at the pan.

I come back with some pajama bottoms I have never worn in my life, a T-shirt I wouldn't be caught dead in, and a fur-lined hooded top I actually quite like.

"Here." I hold out the clothes to Angus who, to my mortification, is no longer watching the pan on the stove but instead peering at the walls.

"*Oh*," he breathes, almost as if he doesn't want me to hear him.

Fuck, I forgot.

I collect myself enough to roll my eyes. "Don't tell me you've never read any erotic fiction before?"

I actually hear him swallow. He shakes his head and mumbles, “No. Not even… watched any porn. Dad would’ve killed me.”

“Well, you’re not staying in my kitchen all night to make up for it,” I say matter-of-factly. “Take these through to Oskar.”

“Why did you put it all over your kitchen walls?” he asks, carefully taking the clothes from me.

“Why not? Beautiful writing pleases me wherever it is,” I say as coolly as I can, moving back to my position in front of the cooker so that I can pretend it’s the heat of the flames that’s making me flushed.

The food is ready and doesn’t need stirring, but stirring it gives me something to focus on, something to do with my hands.

“Oh… you didn’t like the coffee,” he says quietly.

Swinging round, I catch his disappointed expression before he can hide it.

Mentally I kick myself for leaving everything sitting on the table, exactly where it was when I left for work this morning.

Sighing, I turn the cooker off. I never know what to say, but right now I feel like I should be as honest with him as I can. He looks upset.

“Angus, I just couldn’t work out why you’d brought me breakfast. Last night shouldn’t have happened. I shouldn’t have let it. It was a mistake. But you did *nothing* wrong.”

I find myself staring at his neck, but his jumper comes up too high to see the skin I marked, the only evidence of our brief encounter.

He shrugs self-consciously.

“I just wanted you to….”

He doesn’t finish the sentence, but he doesn’t have to. I know what he was going to say; it’s written all over his face.

I do like you, a traitorous voice in my head cries. *I like you so fucking much.* I close my eyes trying to shut it out, trying to clamp down on the feelings that threaten to rise up.

Briskly, I grab a plate and dish up the food onto it. “I’m going to take this through to Oskar,” I say without looking back.

Chapter 3

IT IS eight o'clock on a Sunday morning, and yet I have work in half an hour. It just seems wrong. Sundays are for never getting out of bed. Except I haven't got a bed right now… Oskar is in it. He crashed out almost as soon as he'd wolfed down the food I made last night, and he's still sleeping.

I've been brooding at the kitchen table since dawn. I didn't sleep well on the couch—it's comfortable, but I couldn't stop the stupid chatter in my head. I still can't.

How can I leave a stranger alone in my flat while I go to work? How did I end up with a stranger sleeping in my flat in the first place?

I still haven't been down to see Eleanor.

I take one last gulp of coffee, then grab my keys and make my way downstairs.

Although I always bring it with me, I never use my spare key to open Eleanor's door in the morning. It just seems rude somehow, so instead I knock softly.

I'm not surprised when it's Angus who opens the door.

"Hey," he says, doing the smile-look-down-blush thing that makes me want to reach out and tilt his head up so I can see the beautiful gray of his eyes. "How's Oskar this morning?"

"Sleeping," I say wryly, feeling a lot less than wry about it.

"Aren't you working in a bit?"

I sigh. "Yeah. Maybe he'll sleep all day."

But I know how unlikely that is and how far more likely it is he'll go poking round my flat. Maybe he'll work out I have nothing valuable to steal and hobble off to wherever he came from. Here's hoping.

Eleanor is sitting at the table, her hands wrapped round a mug of steaming coffee. She looks up as I walk in, but her blue eyes are a little unfocused, and she doesn't seem quite herself.

Angus stands behind her head and mouths, "*Temazepam*."

Right.

She grips my hand as I sit down. The gesture reminds me of my nan when she was dying and scared she wouldn't ever see any of us again. But Eleanor is not an old lady.

"They're going to come back," Eleanor says quietly, her nails digging into my skin. "We've got to be ready. Angus is going to get the bars for the windows put on today." I look over at Angus perched on the arm of the couch, fiddling with the threaded leather bracelet wrapped round his wrist. Beneath the collar of his loose gray T-shirt, I can now see the faint bruise-colored mark on his neck. I wonder if Eleanor has noticed. I can't stop staring at it.

"Why don't you wait until I get home after work, and I'll have a look at the windows, and we'll see how you feel about it then," I say, using all my willpower to bring my focus back to Eleanor, where it should be.

Bars on the windows will make this flat into even more of a prison.

"I see their shadows outside my window. They're going to come back. We've got to be ready. Help me get ready, Josh," she pleads.

I can see why Angus gave her the temazepam. I know if he hadn't, she wouldn't just be sitting here pleading, she would be ceaselessly checking the windows were still locked, the doors bolted. The curtains would be opened, then closed in a restless cycle of desperate paranoia.

Angus gets up and comes over to hold her other hand. Like a kid seeking comfort, he rests his head on her shoulder and presses her hand into his hair. I want to tell him what she can't—that he doesn't have to be scared—but anxiety is like a disease, infecting everyone around it. I make a decision to talk to him later about calling the doctor out again. At least then we can be prepared for the worst.

TODAY IT'S just me and Emma at the shop. Soren isn't working. I don't normally work with Emma as she only works on a Sunday, but the other Sunday girl, Lindsay, is on holiday and Soren and I are alternating the holiday cover. Already I know far more than I want to about Emma's student lifestyle, as unfortunately Sundays are quiet and Emma is talkative.

"I have such a hangover. Make me a cup of tea, Josh," she pleads, coming to stand so close behind me for a moment, I can feel her not insignificant breasts touching my back. She's always brushing past me, tactile as a cat after some food.

It's not long after we've opened up. When it's quiet like this (completely dead in fact—there is not a soul in the shopping center yet), we can sneak hot drinks out onto the shop floor.

I think about saying no, but at least if I'm in the kitchen, she has to be out in the shop dealing with any customers that might appear, and she won't be talking to me. It's not that I don't like talking to her. It's just I am a whirling mess of anxiety this morning, worrying about Eleanor and Angus and what Oskar is getting up to in my flat, and I don't want to talk to anyone, especially not about any of that. A few minutes making tea might give me some space to calm down.

"Did you go out last night?" she asks as I hand her a cup of tea and sit on the unoccupied chair behind the cash register while she sits on the narrow shelf next to it. Her skirt has ridden almost all the way up her thighs.

Thing with Emma is, she thinks everyone under thirty lives the student lifestyle if they're not tied down by kids. The whole "drink-party-sleep-repeat, possibly attend a lecture if not too hungover" thing is not my thing at all.

"Nope."

"Do you *ever* go out, Josh?" she asks absently, putting the tea down and pulling at her long blonde plait that hangs over her shoulder and fiddling with the shiny strands of hair. She has perhaps the longest blondest hair I have ever seen.

"Nope." I take a sip of tea, wondering when she's going to remember that she's asked me this before, a few times now. She probably thinks I'm the dullest person alive. Maybe she's right.

"Are you gay?"

The question comes out of nowhere.

I choke on my tea, spitting most of the liquid in my mouth back into the cup. Disgusted, I put the cup down on the counter and wipe my lips. She has never asked me *that* before.

"Why do you ask?" I croak.

Emma is watching me critically.

"I hit on you *all* the time. And I know you don't have a girlfriend, so you're either completely stupid, asexual, or gay. And gay seems more likely than the other two."

"Or you just might not be my *type*," I offer.

I'm not saying it to offend her. But heck, I'm pretty offended myself, though I'm not sure why.

Emma raises a neat eyebrow and hitches her skirt down a fraction. I'm guessing she doesn't get told she's not someone's type too often.

"Because, let me guess, your type doesn't have breasts and a vagina?"

Thankfully she looks more amused than upset.

"Do you really hit on me? Like when?" Now I'm curious. I can't imagine being so oblivious. Was the skirt thing hitting on me? Is that what girls do?

"You're evading the question. I'm right, aren't I?"

I shift uncomfortably, feeling boxed into a corner. Luckily this is the moment the first customer of the day chooses to walk through the door, and I leap up to go be sales assistant of the year or whatever, though I can feel Emma glaring frustratedly at my back.

By lunchtime I can't avoid her anymore.

"So what if I am?" I sigh, walking over to her when the shop is empty.

I don't qualify it—Emma knows exactly what I'm talking about.

Standing up, she leans over the cash register—where she has been sitting the whole morning because her head hurts too much to move, apparently—her ample breasts resting on the keyboard, and hugs me. It's as if I've told her the most amazing secret.

"We are *so* going to get you set up with someone!" she whispers conspiratorially, and I can't suppress the shiver of dread that courses through my body.

As the day progresses, I begin to wish I'd thought quicker and told Emma I already had a boyfriend, as she dismisses every comment I make about not wanting to meet anyone and about not being interested in a relationship. But the worst thing is, every time she asks me if I have a type, it's like there is some faulty wiring in my brain and all I can think about is Angus—the weight of his thick dark hair in my hands when I kissed him, the stunning gray of his eyes.

Suffice it to say the rest of my day at work is dire, though I don't find myself worrying about anything else until I'm on my way home.

I drive too quickly and then sit in the car outside my flat for another five minutes, staring up at the brightly lit top-floor windows, wondering what is going on in my living room and wishing nothing was going on and no one was there so I could go home and be alone.

In the downstairs hallway, I catch the faint scent of bleachy disinfectant. It's unusual, as Eleanor is the only one who ever cleans the communal hallway, and since the robbery she has not even been anywhere near her own front door, never mind the communal one.

After giving Eleanor's door a quick knock and not getting any response, I use my key. As soon as I push the door open, I am overwhelmed by bleach fumes. The whole flat reeks of it.

I can see Eleanor in the kitchen, cloth in her hand, bucket at her side. She is still in her dressing gown. All the food and cooking utensils are out of the cupboards and stacked up on the table. In the living room, Eleanor has rearranged the furniture to form a barricade across the window: the sofa is pushed back so it's right under the windowsill with the two armchairs piled on top of it. All the lights in the flat are on, the curtains drawn.

Swallowing my shock, I call out to let Eleanor know I'm there before walking down the hallway into the kitchen.

Without letting her gaze linger on me, she opens her mouth and says something, but her words tumble out too quickly for me to be sure what it is.

The whole situation is a little disconcerting. I step toward her and touch her arm, but she flinches away and looks at me with a feverish gleam in her eyes.

"Where's Angus?" I ask gently, looking round, perhaps expecting to find him cowering in a corner, unable to deal with this new twist in her behavior.

But she doesn't respond. She carries on wiping down the already clean cupboards, over and over as if she will find what she needs in the repetition of the movement.

"Eleanor?" I say again.

When she looks at me, I get the feeling she's not really seeing me. It's frightening. I know what it feels like to be so lost inside yourself nothing outside of you makes sense.

I don't want to leave her, but I need Angus here. I need to talk to him about calling someone because Eleanor can't go on like this. We can't keep pretending she'll be okay, that she *is* okay, because she isn't. She needs help.

ON THE way out of her flat, I notice Angus's coat is hanging up in the hall. It's doubtful he's gone outside anywhere without it in this cold. I pull Eleanor's door closed and, feeling as though my legs are filled with wet sand, walk upstairs to my flat.

I can hear their voices from halfway down the stairs. Oskar is talking, and every so often Angus joins in and laughs. It makes me realize I've never really heard Angus laugh much, apart from the other night when he was drunk in my flat.

I doubt he's going to be feeling like laughing in a minute.

God, I wish we didn't have to do this.

My door is unlocked, and for a second or two, I stand in the doorway listening to their conversation. They seem to be getting on really well. I don't want to admit it, but I'm kind of jealous, though I'm not sure why. And then I realize what they're talking about, and I lean against the wall, my stomach lurching nauseously.

"I wish things were different.... We got close once... but he's not really into me...." Angus's voice is so low I can barely catch his words.

"There are plenty of other guys who would be. Other guys that are right here, right—"

I step into the living room, dragging a smile on my face and acting as if I haven't just heard Oskar making a pass at Angus.

I'm not being weirdly possessive, and there is no other reason for me making my entrance right then other than Oskar is just not suitable. We know nothing about him. It's likely he's an addict—I picked him up outside Soren's dealer's house, after all. He's probably dying for his fix right now. Angus does not need that sort of person in his life.

"Hey!" Angus shoots to his feet off the sofa, looking both shocked and strangely elated to see me. He shoves his hands in his pockets as though he doesn't know what else to do with them. I watch the way his Adam's apple bobs up and down as he swallows and the faint but utterly disconcerting blush that rushes across his cheeks.

"I was, erm, just keeping Oskar company." He gives me a meaningful look. "I should, erm, probably go now." He points to the door as if I don't know what direction he means to go in and then, with his head down, walks straight past me.

Oskar raises his eyebrow, looking faintly amused. I shake my head and reach out, touching Angus's shoulder before he can disappear.

"Wait a sec," I say softly.

I don't move my hand, and Angus doesn't move away. We don't look at each other, but I can feel his warmth emanating through his T-shirt into my fingertips. The longer I leave my hand there, the more warmth seems to fill me—flooding my bloodstream, pooling in the pit of my stomach.

"How are you doing?" I ask Oskar, staring at the way his cast is propped up on my coffee table. His skin looks sickly pale, though I'm not sure if that's just natural for him, as he looked sickly pale when I first saw him before I ran over his foot.

"My foot hurts like a bitch, but I guess that's to be expected," he sighs.

"Do you need any painkillers?"

I remembered halfway through the morning that I should have left some paracetamol or something out for him. I keep them locked in the bathroom cabinet, but he wouldn't know that. The hospital said last night that he should take painkillers as and when he needed them. I feel guilty as hell about it now.

"It's okay. Angus has been looking after me."

I feel Angus shift—a liquid roll of muscle beneath my palm—and sense he feels uncomfortable.

Oskar folds his arms across his chest. It's a slightly defensive gesture I try not to mirror. I like where my hand is on Angus's shoulder too much right now.

"Um, actually I need to use the phone, but I didn't want to use yours without asking you first."

Charmed by Oskar's consideration, I drop my hand away from Angus to dig my mobile out of my pocket. I hand it to Oskar.

"Call who you need to. I have some things to sort out with Angus. I'll be back in a bit," I say.

Angus is waiting by my front door.

"Come on," I say grimly, brushing past him and making my way back down the stairs.

"What is it?" he calls after me worriedly. "Is it Mum? Is she okay?"

He obviously decides she isn't as, without waiting for me to answer, he jumps down half the stairs and reaches his front door before I do. His shaking hands make hard work of getting his key into the lock.

"Hold on." I put my hand over his. I don't know why. I'm not a tactile person. An impossible-to-control desire to comfort him has temporarily taken over my brain. "I should warn you the flat's a mess and the window's barricaded. How long were you upstairs?"

Angus swallows and looks away. "I didn't mean to stay so long. I like Oskar. I liked talking to him. I haven't spoken to anyone… friends… since…." He stops, wipes his arm across his eyes, and takes a deep breath. He's so immediately emotional—he reacts so quickly to things—it's utterly disarming. "I know she's not okay, Josh. I just want everything to be normal. I know I shouldn't've—"

I pull him into my arms. It's such a bad idea, but it feels like the only thing I can do right now. I feel him grip my coat in his hands and sob against me, and it's all I can do to stop myself from pulling him closer, holding him as tightly as I can, telling him lies like it'll be okay, that I'll make sure it's okay, that I'll look after him. Things I can't promise. Things, I tell myself, I don't even want to.

He smells like heaven. The sensation of his body against mine makes my knees weak.

I have to push him away. Though I make sure I'm gentle.

I hand him a tissue out of the pocket of my coat and wait while he wipes his eyes and blows his nose.

"Let's go and sort this out."

I give his hand one last reassuring squeeze, and we open the door.

Chapter 4

IT TAKES the two of us to stop Eleanor cleaning. Gently I take the cloth and the bottle of bleach out of her hands even though she resists me. Then Angus removes them far out of sight. Eleanor's hands are red and raw-looking. The bleach fumes are making me feel woozy.

"We should open a window," I say to Angus.

I lead Eleanor to sit down in one of the hard-backed dining chairs as Angus scrambles over the piled-up furniture to drag the curtains back and open one of the living room windows.

For a while after that, the three of us sit at the table—Eleanor sagging in my arms, Angus looking at us miserably.

"What now?" he asks in a croaked whisper.

"Eleanor?" I say softly.

She doesn't respond. She is barely moving. Only the faint but rapid rise and fall of her chest indicates she's breathing. I've seen a few people enter catatonic states in my life, but I can't bear to see Eleanor like this. She's been like a mother to me.

"Help me take her to bed," I say to Angus.

I can't have this conversation with Eleanor sitting here between us but not taking part in it—it feels wrong somehow.

Between us we carry her to the bedroom and lay her gently on the bed. I leave the door open, so if she calls out, however faintly, we will hear her.

I don't know if how she feels is in any way similar to how I felt all those years ago. If it is, I wish I'd done something to help her sooner. Being trapped in your own head ruled by anxiety is hell.

"Did your mum ever tell you anything about my past?" I ask once we are back in the kitchen, sitting down at the table.

Angus nods, concentrating on the deep gouges that scar the dark wood of the old dining table, his hair obscuring much of his face. I'm not sure how much she would have told him about my time in hospital, but he doesn't look as though he wants to talk to me about it anyway. He probably suspects what I'm about to say.

"Did she tell you I was sectioned?"

Again, Angus gives a reluctant nod. It's hard to talk about this, and even harder when the person you're talking to doesn't want to listen. I'm not even sure he fully understands what being sectioned means—what being compulsorily committed to a psychiatric hospital means.

"Those years I spent in and out of hospital were the darkest of my life, but only because I was depressed." He won't look at me. "I would have felt like that wherever I was. If I was on a beach in Barbados or on the fucking moon, it would have made no difference. Nothing I could have done on my own would have made any difference. The only thing that helped me was the drugs they gave me, and the ECT. I had a chemical imbalance in my brain. Things like that just don't go away. Sometimes you have to do something about them, even if it seems hard."

Angus glances at me sidelong.

"I would never suggest we call someone and get your mum sectioned. I think we should get her assessed, though. I think there are treatments available that can help her. I don't think we're doing her any favors by doing nothing, Angus. She's getting worse. She's suffered from anxiety for a long time, and this has just tipped the scales. Getting her addicted to temazepam is not going to help her in the long run. Those sorts of drugs don't deal with her anxiety—they just mask it. It will become just another thing she's dependent on."

I hate talking about Eleanor like this, but I'm not sure she's even aware of anything right now.

"I know. But what if they do section her?" he says in a hoarse whisper, looking up. His eyes are glassy, and I can see he's biting his cheek in an effort not to cry. "What do I do then? Where do I go?"

"Look, we'll deal with that if it comes to it. This is your home. You should be able to stay here."

"How?" He swallows. "I have no money. I don't want to go back to my dad's. I can't do that again." His voice breaks, and he sags forward, resting his head on the table as though he doesn't want me to see him crying this time. I reach across the table to stroke his thick, dark hair. "I've never been on my own.... I want her to be okay, Josh. I just want her to be okay," he mumbles into the tabletop.

"I know," I say gently.

We find a number for an emergency psychiatric team in one of the leaflets the police left behind. Angus takes the phone from me and walks to the far side of the living room to make the call.

I'm surprised. I was prepared to be the one to talk to them. I didn't expect him to want to deal with this at all.

I boil the kettle to make a cup of tea for us both and start putting away all the food Eleanor took out of the cupboards. I am trying not to listen to Angus's side of the conversation, but it's hard—harder because he's so obviously upset. I concentrate on what I'm doing in an effort to quash the stupid urge to go and sit with him, to be his shoulder to cry on. If I did that, I can't imagine anything good coming of it, just confused feelings and mixed messages. These urges that make me want to comfort him and be there for him are throwing me off balance. I don't know what to do for the best anymore.

Instead I try to think about something else. Thinking about Oskar alone in my flat is a good distraction. Perhaps he's managed to call someone and find somewhere else to stay. I don't want to chuck him out, but I can't help selfishly wanting my flat to myself again either.

"They'll be here before ten," Angus says, putting the phone down on the table.

He runs his hands through his hair, looking completely washed-out. His complexion is drawn and pale.

"Tonight?"

Angus nods.

They must think it's serious.

"Will you be here when they come?" He flicks his gaze up at me hopefully and chews his lower lip.

"I should go check on Oskar and sort out some food, but… yeah, of course I'll come back down."

I reach out and squeeze his shoulder reassuringly before I can stop myself. Holding my gaze, he gives me a grateful smile. Only it's not just grateful. Angus doesn't hide anything. He's so straightforward. My heart is beating like a broken drum. It suddenly hits me how easy it would be for someone to fall for him. How unfair on him it would be if that someone was broken and not good enough—and this time I'm not thinking about Oskar.

I hand him his tea and quickly turn around and walk away.

"WHAT'S GOING on?" Oskar asks as I slump down in the green velvet armchair opposite him.

Sighing, I shake my head. I don't want to talk about it.

My phone is on the coffee table. Oskar has obviously finished making his phone calls. Leaning forward, I pick it up and put it back in my pocket.

"I've got somewhere to stay from tomorrow," he tells me with a kind of forced brightness to his tone. He won't look at me.

In the warm glow of the lamp, I notice he has a not unattractive band of freckles across his nose.

I sigh.

Between running over Oskar's foot and what I've just suggested Angus do downstairs, I'm feeling pretty much like the wielder of doom. It's a pretty crap feeling too.

"A friend?"

"Sort of," he mumbles, his brown eyes flicking up to look at the ceiling, his good leg jogging up and down, making the floorboard beneath his foot creak.

Although I think he's older than Angus and far more worldly, there is still something innocent about him. Some denial of the adult world in his actions.

"You don't have to stay anywhere else. Look, I ran over and broke your foot. The least I can do is offer you a place to stay until you are okay again," I reply wearily.

It might be the last thing I think I *want* to do, but I force myself to at least offer him this. I want to be a good person. I just don't suspect I am.

"Josh, I know you hate me being here. And you haven't even got a TV." He tries to give me a smile, but it fades too fast. He's just a kid like Angus. A kid who accepts bad things happen to him and thinks that's how his life has to be. I don't know what to say.

I change the subject. "Are you hungry?"

Before I left this morning, I made Oskar a sandwich and put it on the bedside cabinet so he would see it when he woke up. From the empty plate next to him, it looks as though he's eaten it, but he must be starving by now. He's thin enough as it is.

I hardly wait for his reply before I'm in the kitchen, seeing what I can rustle up with what I have in my fridge—a little fresh pasta, some bacon, cream, and frozen peas. I decide to make enough for Angus too.

Cooking is not something I ever imagined I would enjoy, but strangely, I do enjoy it. Even stranger, given my solitary tendencies, is the fact that I seem to enjoy cooking for other people.

The cooker has a built-in radio. I bought it off eBay, and I've never seen another one like it. The instructions are all in Swedish. I turn the radio on in between frying the bacon and putting a pan of water on to boil. I don't listen to music. Only stories, plays, poetry slams, anything where words are spoken passionately, incessantly. It brings me great comfort, release almost—catharsis for all the feelings I don't let myself feel too deeply. All the words I don't say. The channels are all bookmarked and I flick through them until something catches my interest.

"THANK YOU," Oskar says, his eyes lighting up as I hand him a dish piled high with pasta. His reaction is too genuinely enthusiastic to be fake. It makes me think he's not had much kindness in his life, and I feel all the worse about the past two days.

He deserves a better nurse than me.

I retreat back into the kitchen where I left my and Angus's portions warm in the pan. I pile up another plate for Angus and take it downstairs to him.

"This is amazing," Oskar calls as I pass the living room.

I give him a small smile. I think he's trying to make friends, but I don't think I can bridge the gap between us—my guilt is too great.

"FOR ME?" Angus asks, standing in his doorway and looking surprised as I hold out the plate of food.

"Eat it quick. It's not so nice cold. How is Eleanor?"

"Sleeping," Angus says, taking a deep breath, which he then exhales shakily.

"I'll come back down in a bit."

I touch his arm, no longer sure if the reassurance is for him or for me.

I know he's staring after me as I make my way back upstairs.

I wish I didn't like it.

OSKAR HAS almost ploughed his way through the whole plateful by the time I sit down in the living room with him to eat mine. I hand him a cold beer and take a deep draught of my own. Today has been a long day and it's not over yet.

"Can I ask you something?" he says, putting his empty plate down and then cradling his beer.

I look up, thinking, *That depends on whether you expect an answer or not.*

"I just want to ask you...." He winces, shifting in his seat uncomfortably. "It's never easy to ask someone... and I don't want you to get the wrong idea... I mean, you're probably not. It's just... and I know I've only spoken to him for an afternoon...." I wait for him to spit it out. "I like Angus," he says eventually. "A lot."

"That's not a question," I reply between mouthfuls of pasta. Even though I'm well aware of what the question might be now he's said that. It seems to be the day for them. No one has cared that I might be gay for the past five years, and now two people ask me in one day.

Even so, without having heard Angus and Oskar's conversation earlier, I would probably be thrown by Oskar's admission and not know what to say. Now I get to play it cool and pretend I have a heart of stone.

Oskar's gaze flicks down to his hands. With his thin, sharp features and large brown eyes, he's not unattractive, and everything he's said and done so far indicates that, despite his air of distrust, he has a good heart underneath it all. But like he says, only a fool trusts anyone, and Oskar remains a mostly unknown quantity.

"Is there anything going on between you? Because I wouldn't... if there was," he sort of whispers.

"No, there is nothing going on," I say. Though the words come out sounding much more abrupt than I mean them to, and I get the distinct feeling that that wasn't what I wanted to say at all.

We finish our meal in awkward silence.

AT NINE forty-five I go downstairs. I knock lightly, and Angus lets me in, looking more than a little stressed. I sit down in one of the dining chairs while he paces anxiously.

"Come and sit down," I say gently. And surprisingly he does.

The plate I brought his food down on is empty on the work surface. I'm pleased. I wasn't sure he'd eat anything.

"We need to be prepared for what they might say," I tell him.

Angus nods stiffly as though he is preparing himself for the absolute worst. He glances at the kitchen clock.

"It's going to be okay." I grip his hand even as I berate myself for telling stupid lies. Even though I wish I *could* make everything okay. "Just be honest with them."

We are expecting the psychiatric team at any moment, yet we both nearly jump to the ceiling when the doorbell rings.

Angus gets up to answer it. Two women are with him when he returns. They are psychiatric nurses. They introduce themselves as Amy Flowers and Ella King, and explain they are qualified to assess patients, and if a doctor is needed for any decision then they just have to make a call. I know they mean if Eleanor needs to be sectioned.

I glance at Angus, expecting him to be overwhelmed and wishing this wasn't happening, but mostly he looks… relieved.

"So, tell me about your mum's behavior," Amy says to Angus once we're sitting back down at the table.

Angus swallows and then tells them about last week's burglary and how anxious it has left Eleanor.

The burglary has left them both anxious—only Angus's anxiety is entirely proportional.

Under the table, I rub his leg reassuringly. If he notices, I can't tell.

"Eleanor has suffered from some level of anxiety ever since I've known her, and she's been agoraphobic for a number of years now," I add when he's finished speaking.

Angus widens his eyes at me as if to say *Why on earth would you tell them that*? But I want Eleanor to get the help she deserves. Now we've finally made the call, it's as though I can at last admit how bad things have become, and this week has been… heartbreaking. Eleanor's confidence in everything—shattered.

I can't help thinking I should have talked Eleanor into getting help for her anxiety years ago. I feel so guilty that it's probably my own skewed opinion of what constitutes normal behavior and what doesn't, and perhaps my own fears of mental health departments that have kept me from dealing with this in the best way. Her life could have been so much better than this. *Should* have been.

"Can we speak to Eleanor now?" Ella asks.

I stay sitting down while Angus gets up and shows them through to Eleanor's room. Their low voices drift through the flat's thin walls, though I can't hear what they're saying. I pick at the trails of wax on the table's surface, thinking about Angus when I should be thinking about Eleanor. When they return, the nurses look as though they have made a decision.

"We're going to recommend Eleanor comes in of her own free will as an inpatient. I will contact the hospital and leave the details with you," Ella says.

Angus chews his lip and looks at me.

It strikes me that they can't have taken her agoraphobia into consideration—the fact that she's not left the flat for the past few years.

"How?" I frown. "Did Eleanor agree to go in?"

"No. She wasn't particularly responsive. You will need to speak to her in the morning."

Without making it obvious to anyone but Angus, I roll my eyes.

"What if Angus was here on his own. Would he be expected to convince and then somehow get an extremely anxious and agoraphobic woman to hospital?"

"If we deem a patient is a threat to others or a threat to themselves, we will arrange immediate ambulance transportation. We agree Eleanor needs treatment, but her participation is entirely voluntary, and therefore she needs to make her own way to the hospital."

Angus leans back against the kitchen wall and squeezes his eyes shut as though he just wants to disappear or at least make all this shit go away. The relief he displayed earlier is gone.

"This is ridiculous," I say, shaking my head and standing up. Ella seems to be the one in charge, so I speak directly to her. "You need to send someone out tomorrow morning to help us. And it needs to be someone who has experience in dealing with this sort of situation. Eleanor needs help. She needs treatment for her anxiety, but she also needs it to be respected. I will not force her to do something that terrifies the hell out of her, and you cannot expect her *son* to do that either."

Ella sighs. She looks at me for a good long moment as if weighing up how much trouble I'm going to be if she says no, and then she takes out her phone. "I will see what I can do. If she would perhaps prefer to be sedated, I can send someone out to talk to her about that."

I nod okay.

I DON'T sleep much. Mostly I worry about Eleanor. The thought of her in the hospital brings back so many echoes of my past. It's not a trigger for anything. I have coping mechanisms that let me deal with things like this—coping mechanisms that stop all feelings going too deep, that keep all hurt at a surface level, like a superficial graze that will never need stitches. *Don't feel anything, don't let anything go too deep inside, and you'll be okay* is the rule I live by. But I know things are beginning to slip beneath my defenses.

I worry about Angus too, though I try not to. The way he dealt with the situation tonight, calling the nurses, acting instead of ignoring, made me realize something. All along I've thought of him as this helpless, unworldly kid, but now I'm beginning to think I might have been wrong.

Curled uncomfortably on the sofa, I doze off just before dawn. I wake when Oskar uses the bathroom and the flushing of the toilet permeates my dream.

I'm shocked when I see it's 9:00 a.m. I don't have to be into work until eleven, but I want to be downstairs when the nurse comes for Eleanor, and I meant to be awake long before now. Oskar has gone back to sleep, splayed out possessively across my comfortable bed, and I don't want to disturb him just to get dressed. Still wearing the clothes I slept in, I quietly make my way downstairs.

Angus's face is a mask when he opens the door. As soon as I step inside, he leans into my personal space, hesitating for a brief moment before resting his forehead on my shoulder. The contact is warm. Angus is warm. His breath washes over my skin. There is something about being breathed on so closely like this that turns me on. My dick is getting hard. I wish it wasn't, and I wish I'd taken a shower and put some deodorant on, because breathing me in can't be a real pleasant experience for Angus right now.

"They've taken her," he whispers.

My desire dies.

"When?"

Leaning back against the door, I pull Angus into my arms, feeling him melt against me.

"About half an hour ago," he murmurs.

"You should have come and got me," I say thickly, my lips against his hair. He really should have. "Was she okay?"

"Yeah," he breathes, but he doesn't elaborate further.

I really hope she was okay. It still hurts to think of her in the state she was in last night, but I don't press Angus any further as I sense he doesn't want to talk about it.

We stand like that for so long, I begin to lose circulation in my arm from where it is pressed between Angus and the door, but I don't want to move.

And I don't want to think about why not.

I COOK Angus a bit of breakfast and sit with him while he eats it. There is not much food in his fridge, and I make a mental note to go shopping later.

"I've got to work in a bit. Are you going to be okay?"

Angus pulls a resigned face and sighs. "I'll go for a long run. I'll be fine."

"It's probably best that you don't tell anyone about Eleanor going into hospital for now."

"Because of the flat and stuff?"

I nod even though that's not the reason I was thinking of. I'm more worried about Angus's dad finding out and then pressuring

Angus to go back and live with him. I just don't want to bring that subject up.

"They said we could go see her tomorrow if she's settled in," he says quietly as though he can't speak any louder without his voice cracking.

I look away and nod. Angus doesn't need to know the rush of warmth his including me like this causes.

"Just let me know the times, and we'll go."

OSKAR IS dressed in his own now clean clothes and hobbling around my flat by the time I get back upstairs. I only have a few minutes to get dressed and leave for work.

"I'm getting picked up in a little while," he tells me as I hunt around trying to find my wallet.

I stop. As he stands in the doorway to the kitchen, the morning sunlight floods the space behind him, surrounding him with light. I stare at him for a moment, caught in the brightness.

"You really don't have to go." Suddenly I want to push it. I think he should stay until he's healed. I think I should do this one good thing. "I mean, if you have somewhere better where they're going to look after you, fine, but don't just go because you think you have to. I'm just naturally miserable and bad-tempered, but it doesn't mean you shouldn't stay here. I'm not completely heartless."

I don't think, anyway. I frown.

Oskar raises an eyebrow. "I wouldn't say you were bad-tempered, just a bit… antisocial."

"Thanks," I say, raising my eyebrow, though I give him a smile.

"It's okay. I should… go. I can walk… sort of… and my foot should be better in a few weeks."

He looks resolute.

I keep a bit of money in a book in the hall. For emergencies. Before I leave, I take it out, put it in an envelope, and place it on the coffee table next to where Oskar is now resting his foot.

"I'd feel better if you had this," I say. "It's not going to make me feel less guilty about anything, but I want you to take it." It's not much, a few hundred pounds maybe. I didn't want to count it. "Just pull the door to when you leave."

Oskar gives me a grateful look, and I know he stares after me when I leave.

AFTER THE first customer of the day leaves, Soren just about bounces across the shop floor toward me—looking far too happy to be at work, as usual.

"Josh, you've got a face like a wet weekend. What's up?" he asks.

People like Soren shouldn't be allowed in the morning.

"Eleanor's anxiety got worse. She's in hospital." I take a bit of paperwork out of the plastic folder in front of me and then take twice as long putting it back in, waiting for Soren to say "I told you so."

"This is your neighbor, right?" Soren leans over the cash register I'm sitting behind, his light blue eyes scrutinizing me. Once again I am reminded how disgustingly attractive he is.

"Yep."

I dig around under the cash register for any stray receipts or rubbish. Perhaps if I look like I've got something to do, he'll go away.

"So, she'll get some help now, right?"

Soren puts a hand out and squeezes my shoulder. I force myself not to freeze, but I'm shocked. Casual contact always shocks me, especially from other men. Repeatedly I tell myself I'm just not a tactile person, but I think it's more than that. I think it's perhaps related to my determination not to feel anything too deeply, not to become involved.

"Hopefully," I murmur.

"How's her son taking it?"

"Okay."

But I don't want to talk about Angus. I'm filled with such weirdly protective feelings every time I even think about him, and I'm trying really hard *not* to think about him.

"So, I hear you and Emma had a little chat yesterday."

Soren changes the subject faster than the fucking wind. For a moment I am a little lost, and then I remember. Fuck. Emma is best friends with Lucy, Soren's girlfriend. Emma has probably announced to the whole world that I'm gay by now. Not that I particularly care that everyone knows. I've never hidden it, but I've never broadcast it either. I'd just rather it not be the focus of attention.

I hold Soren's gaze, wondering if that was why he touched me just now—if it was some weird reassurance that he doesn't care.

"I've known you were gay since forever," he says softly, flicking his damn lip ring with his tongue and smiling.

How? I wonder, but I'm not going to ask. I'm hardly obvious. I'd always thought I'd been careful not to display any inclinations. Emma's suggestion that I might be asexual is closer to how I imagine I appear.

"I've had a crush on you since the day I sat in on your interview. When we first met, you tried to hide it, but I could tell you were attracted to me. People have tells, you know."

Tells? I wonder what mine are. I wonder how I give myself away.

I swallow, trying to take in this new information, because it doesn't make sense. Soren, my boss, who is stunning, has a crush on me. "And you're admitting this now because…?"

"I don't know." He shrugs, stepping back. "Thought it might cheer you up. Don't be under the impression I'm going to do anything about it. You're too antisocial, and more importantly, I have a girlfriend."

"Antisocial…." He's the second person today to say that. I guess I shouldn't be offended by the truth.

"Uh-huh. And it's like you're nice to look at and talk to sometimes, but then you get too maudlin and you think *waaay* too much about shit. One day, though, I'm gonna get you to come out with us, and I'll show you what a good time actually is." Grinning, Soren winks at me and goes to annoy the next customer through the door.

Despite not knowing exactly what to think about Soren's revelations, the rest of the day passes pretty quickly, and I find myself being worn down by his constant conviction that I need to get a social life and his promises of a good time if I agree to go out with him and his friends. Finally I do agree. They have a sort of unofficial Christmas celebration happening in a few weeks, which sounds innocuous enough. At least I don't think Soren will try to hook me up with anyone like Emma would—he seems to have no agenda about matchmaking. Soren doesn't interfere in people's lives so much as he needs to know what's going on in them.

A lot can happen in a few weeks, though, so perhaps Soren will have forgotten about his invitation by then.

I STOP at a supermarket on the way home and get some groceries—mostly for Angus, though I get a few bits for myself too. I'm aware Angus is quite capable of shopping for himself, but I want to do this for him. I've been shopping regularly for Eleanor for years now, but since the burglary our routine has, not surprisingly, become out of sync. I wish she'd told me she needed some more food, though. I feel like crap for not noticing—for not thinking.

ANGUS IS sitting on the stairs in the communal hallway when I get back. I wish my heart wouldn't do the stupid speeding-up thing it does when I see him—it makes me feel light-headed.

He grins at me and flicks his gaze away shyly, although there is an awful lot of relief in his expression too when I smile back at him. I suspect he thinks I might not call in to see him now Eleanor's gone.

I hold out a bag of shopping for him. "Your fridge was empty," I say by way of explanation.

Angus takes the bag, peering inside and looking a little stunned.

"Thank you.... Do... you want to come in for a bit?" he asks hesitantly.

I think about sitting in Eleanor's flat with him without Eleanor there—the smell of bleach still permeating the air, and I shake my head.

"I was, um, just going to make a pizza." I suddenly feel incredibly self-conscious. I realize I've never done what I'm about to do before. "I always make too much.... Do you want to put your shopping away and come up?"

Angus stares at me for a moment. "Okay," he says, nodding far too enthusiastically.

"Bring the portable TV if you like. You're not spending the evening reading porn in my kitchen," I add wryly, my confidence growing with Angus's eagerness.

When he smiles, it is luminous. It lights me up brighter than ever. I'm not even sure what my motives are anymore.

Chapter 5

THE NEXT day I take the afternoon off work and we go and see Eleanor. I wondered if Soren would be okay about my taking the time off even though it's short notice—but he didn't bat a beautiful eyelash. He just filled out my holiday form. I think he's starting to understand that Eleanor is like family to me. Every time I see him, Soren acts more and more like a friend. I guess I should probably think of him as one.

The hospital is nothing like the one I was in. This place is all on one level. It's not a maze—it's all open and spread out with windows along every wall that look over the extensive gardens. The winter sun is shining low and bright, and the whole place feels very calm. There is no frenetic atmosphere, no scent of desperation. No darkness here.

Eleanor has a room to herself just off one of the main communal areas. I gesture to Angus that he go in, saying I need to go ask one of the nurses something. I don't. I just think he needs to have a bit of time alone with his mum. Instead I stand by one of the windows staring out at the strange shadows the bare trees cast on the lawn, hoping our decision was the right one and trying not to let the past replay itself in my head.

After half an hour, I go and get three hot chocolates out of the vending machine in the visitors' waiting room. I've no idea what Eleanor and Angus have been talking about, but they shut up and look vaguely guilty when I walk in.

"Josh." Eleanor holds her arms open for me. I put the hot chocolates down on the cabinet beside her so I can hug her tight.

"Are you all right?" I whisper. She looks all right at least. More relaxed. Sitting in an armchair in this neat little room all laid out like a little living room, with a bed in the corner.

"Angus, can you go and ask one of the nurses for another jug of water, please?" Eleanor asks.

Angus rolls his eyes. "If you want me to disappear for a minute so you can talk to Josh, just say so."

There's more affection than annoyance in his tone.

Eleanor hugs me until he's gone, and only then does she pull away. Now she looks shaky again, her gaze darting to the door as if to make sure Angus has really gone.

"Josh, listen to me. I know I shouldn't ask you to do this, but I need you to watch over Angus. You all think I'm so confused and anxious." Eleanor makes a pained sound and starts wringing her hands together over and over. "And I know things have got mixed up, but I've seen them watching in the dark outside the flat, and I know they're waiting. I know they're going to come back. I can't stand the thought of Angus all alone in there. You can't let anything happen to him, Josh. *Please*," she begs me.

I've never seen her look quite this desperate, and the past few days I've seen a lot of how desperate she can get. The movement of her hands is making *me* feel anxious. I'm not sure whether it's best to let her carry on doing it or not. Sometimes people have actions that calm them, and I don't know if this is one of them, but like the other night when she was cleaning over and over, she doesn't seem to be getting any calmer doing it.

"I'm not going to let anything happen to him," I promise her, taking her hands in mine. At first she resists, but then she grips my hands tightly in return.

"You do care about him, don't you? I need someone to look out for him, someone who cares about him."

"Yes," I say honestly. "I promise I won't let anyone hurt him."

Those damn near overwhelming protective urges fill every space inside me, and I realize with dreadful clarity that I would rather die than let anyone hurt Angus.

Crap, I think.

Something makes me turn, and I see Angus's face pressed against the glass. He yawns and holds up a jug of water. I glance at

Eleanor to make sure she's finished what she wanted to talk to me about and beckon him back inside.

Angus puts the jug of water on the table and brushes his hair out of his eyes, tucking long strands of it behind his ears. Briefly he glances between us as if he's trying to figure out what we were talking about. From the meaningful look he gives me, I know he's noticed Eleanor's increased anxiety. Somehow we make an unspoken agreement to spend the rest of the hour trying to distract her and make her laugh in any way possible. I've never had that weird sort of connection with anyone before, where you look at them and sort of know what they're thinking. It's puzzling and exhilarating at the same time.

I'm not good at making people laugh, but Angus is sweet and funny when he's not feeling self-conscious. He tells stories about when he was a little kid. Just stupid stuff like how he never had any willpower to stop himself eating the biscuits and cakes Eleanor used to bake straight from the oven, and how it used to drive Eleanor crazy, thinking she'd made more than she had. Angus would hotfoot it upstairs, burning his hands and mouth to eat whatever he had taken, and when Eleanor pulled the baking tray out from the oven, looking perplexed, he would feel so guilty, he'd just blurt out that he'd eaten them. If there was any chocolate in the house, he'd do the same thing, knowing it was wrong but unable to help himself. And he'd always admit it.

"It was stupid," he says, grinning. "If I didn't have an inbuilt guilt switch, I could have gotten away with loads."

I don't think it sounds stupid at all, just sort of endearing. It makes me wonder what happened to make their family fall so completely apart. Though I know from experience, sometimes these things just happen.

"You can probably guess I was a chubby kid."

Eleanor shakes her head. "It was just puppy fat," she says, looking more relaxed than I've seen her in a long time.

"It's why I started running. So I could eat what I wanted without all the jokes about my size. What I didn't realize was that when you start running or exercising, you don't want to eat unhealthy crap all the time. Probably worked out for the best, though."

I just smile at him, thinking I could listen to him talk all night and sort of wishing I didn't feel that way. I'm almost certain that I'd still find him beautiful whatever size he was. He shines so bright. His lean body turns me on, but only because it is his. I try and push all the conflict I feel deep down inside myself. Eleanor is the one who needs cheering up. Eleanor is the one who needs us.

At the end of the hour, I think Angus has probably made me smile even more than he made Eleanor smile. He looks strangely pleased with himself.

AFTER THE nurse comes to tell us visiting time is over, I make my way outside to the car while Angus says good-bye. Eleanor didn't want us to go, and I didn't want to have to leave her, but I know she needs a moment alone with her son.

I watch the sky grow navy dark. I watch how it swallows the ribbons of pale cloud, the dark enveloping everything. The streetlights ping on, one by one, all around the car park. And the car park empties until there's just me and a few staff cars.

Half an hour later, Angus walks dejectedly to the car, opens the passenger door, and slumps inside.

I put my arm around his shoulders, and he closes his eyes and curls against me the best he can, given there is a gear stick and a hand brake in the way. I stroke my fingers through his hair and try not to think about anything at all.

We don't talk the whole drive home, but as soon as we've pulled over, I reach into the glove compartment and, with an air of determination, hand him the leaflets I picked up from the local college on my way home. Angus stares at them, then at me.

"What are these for?"

"You said the other day you didn't finish your A levels. But you can still get onto a college course if you take a test."

I just want to take his mind off Eleanor, give him something else to focus on.

"It's nearly December. I'd be too far behind if I went back now."

"You could catch up. You can call them, explain the situation with your dad. They might make an exception."

"Even if I did, I can't afford it, Josh. I've got to get a job to pay the rent. Mum won't get housing benefit while she's in hospital. I've checked up on stuff," Angus says quietly and gets out of the car. He leaves the leaflets on the seat behind him and walks up the path toward the house.

"Wait," I call after him.

I pick the leaflets up, lock the car, then run after him. "Look, Eleanor made me promise to look out for you. She left some money with me to pay for stuff like this." This has got to be the weakest lie I have *ever* told. There are so many ways he could find out it's not true.

Angus eyes me dubiously. I can see the war inside him. He really wants to go to college, but because of his dad, he's afraid of it being on someone else's terms. He's afraid it sounds too good to be true, too easy.

But it *should* be easy for him.

"Why don't I give you the money Eleanor gave me, and you decide what to do with it?"

Why on earth do I want to trust him so fucking much? Mentally I calculate how much I can realistically give him. I've got a few hundred in a savings account, nothing else now I've given Oskar my contingency fund.

But I really want him to go back to college. I really think he should have this chance.

I hand him the leaflets again. "Just think about it," I say.

THE NEXT few days pass quickly. We see Eleanor after I finish work every evening, and every evening she pleads with me to take care of him, tells me they're watching, they're coming, that it's not safe. One day I'm sure Angus overhears, but he doesn't say anything.

He calls the college the day after I give him the leaflets. They interview him and tell him he needs to come in and take a test in a few weeks to see if he knows enough to begin the course in January. I think he'll be fine, but Angus insists on using some of the money I told him Eleanor left him to buy some course books. He spends every day studying, working so hard to catch up, it breaks my heart. He must have been utterly crushed when his dad took away his chance at this.

We develop a regular little routine, with Angus spending a large portion of every evening after we've been to see Eleanor, upstairs with me. I cook for him, and we watch TV or he studies, and sometimes we just talk.

ON THURSDAY evening Angus's phone goes off every couple of minutes with a text message while we're eating. I can't help noticing the way he smiles every time he replies.

He catches me staring.

"Oskar," he says, blushing. "He came to see me the day he left. I gave him my number. He's got a phone now."

I take a deep breath and roll my shoulders back, trying to dispel the sudden tightness I feel in my chest. Angus doesn't need to explain himself, especially not to me. I take our empty plates out to the kitchen.

Standing in front of the sink, I close my eyes. *Oskar.* They're pretty much the same age. It makes sense for them to get on well, to like each other. So why does it feel like the worst thing that could possibly happen?

"Are you okay?"

Swallowing, I turn and see Angus looking at me worriedly from the doorway. I guess I've been stood out here for a while.

I force a smile onto my face and nod.

"I wash up. That's the deal, isn't it?" Angus says softly, moving closer. "You cook, and I clean it all away."

I could teach you to cook, I think, watching the way the light catches his hair, highlighting the dark brown with strands of gold. But then, I've no idea whether Angus would want me to. He'd probably prefer to be out with Oskar having fun—whatever that would entail. He's young. He needs a life beyond my flat, his flat, his mum.

"You only like washing up so you can read the walls." I've no idea why I say that. It's as though my mouth has become disengaged from my brain.

"I don't need to read the walls—my imagination is pretty good. Though I have read most of them." He smiles at his feet and shoves his hands deep in his pockets.

Sometimes I wish he'd do something that'd make me like him less, like be moody or selfish or annoying. But he doesn't. Instead everything he does makes me like him more and more. It's fucking terrifying—it's as though I have this thing I don't want growing inside me.

Or perhaps what's terrifying is the knowledge that if someone cut it out, it'd fucking kill me.

It makes me feel so weak.

"Don't ever change," I say softly.

I *am* so weak.

"What?" He looks up, right at me. He has such beautiful eyes. He searches my face, trying to understand me, maybe.

"Nothing." I shake my head.

I wonder if I'm losing it. I wonder if what's really terrifying me is that this situation is what's going to change and I can do nothing to stop it. Sometimes it feels like life is a train crash, and as I career off the rails, all I can do is lock the door to my carriage and curl up with my head between my knees.

"Can I ask you something?" Angus looks around the room as if his question is written somewhere on the walls.

The weaker part of me wants to say *anything*, yet the sensible part of me wants to say *no*. I restrain myself from muttering any response and just sort of nod.

"Did you write some of these?"

I turn away and twist the tap on so hard, the water splashes all over the sink, my jumper, even the floor. I lean my whole weight against the sink. I let the sink hold me up. For a moment I close my eyes, listening to the rush of water.

Shakily I turn the tap down so that it's not gushing so violently.

I really don't know how to answer Angus's question. I really don't want to answer it at all. Why did he ask me that? How does he know?

Because yes, I wrote some of these. But I can't bear to think of Angus reading my fantasies and knowing it's me who's written them—because that is exactly what the few things I wrote are. Can he not see this is an answer I can't give him? It would be like giving him a free pass inside my head. And I'm ashamed. Ashamed that he's revealed my secret. I don't know why I feel like this, but I've never felt so exposed.

Thankfully Angus doesn't push it.

I hear him walk back into the living room, and I wash up in soapy silence.

FRIDAY NIGHT Angus seems reluctant to go back to his flat. It's gone eleven, and I'm exhausted. A few weeks ago, I probably would have just told him to go home, that I wanted to go to bed, but somehow I can't do that anymore. Somehow our interactions have become a lot more complicated.

He's curled on the sofa, shoes kicked off on the floor beside him, watching some inane comedy program. The canned laughter is really beginning to grate on my nerves, and Angus doesn't seem to be enjoying it much.

"Angus?" I say softly, looking up from the page I've read about fifteen times now. "You okay?"

He nods, chewing his lip, his gaze fixed on the screen. I close my book and put it down on the floor. I go for the not so subtle and sigh before picking up the television controller and turning off the TV.

Angus closes his eyes. For a minute we sit in silence.

"You're going to think I'm as paranoid as my mum… I just… I thought I saw something earlier outside the window. I know it was probably nothing, but I don't feel safe down there," he admits eventually.

"I don't think you're paranoid, Angus."

This has to be a reaction to what he overheard at the hospital, to Eleanor panicking.

"Do you want me to come downstairs with you for a bit?"

"No. It's okay." Reluctantly he gets up and picks his shoes up off the floor. "I know it's stupid."

IT'S SATURDAY, and Angus has been up here since I got off work earlier this afternoon. Sometimes I find myself just watching him. Most of the time I'm careful that he doesn't notice, but today he glances up and sees me standing in the doorway. It's too late to back away or pretend I was just doing anything other than what I am doing.

"I should go and get ready," Angus says, stretching his arms above his head, then getting up from my desk where he's been sitting studying for the past couple of hours.

"Ready? You're going out tonight?"

I was going to ask him if he wanted to eat with me again. I kind of expected him to say yes. It's weird, but I'm beginning to get so used to his company, to welcome it even. Crave it, perhaps.

"Oskar invited me out. We're going to grab something to eat and then go to the cinema, I think," Angus says, shrugging awkwardly.

"He likes you."

The words just come out.

Angus blushes. "Is there anything wrong with that?" he asks quietly.

There is a quiet challenge in his question that I try to ignore, and yet I think about it long after Angus has gone downstairs to get ready.

I LISTEN out for him leaving, for his door to open, then close, his footsteps on the path. But I don't hear anything for an hour, so I wander down and sit on the stairs, thinking perhaps he's already left. He hasn't. About fifteen minutes later, he steps out of his flat looking and smelling fresh and newly scrubbed. His skin glows pink; his eyes are alive, excited maybe. He's somehow managed to flatten down his wild curls, though a few have sprung free, and that makes me smile a little. *I'm trying*, I think. *I'm trying so hard.*

Angus bites his lip and looks puzzled when he sees me. I don't know why I'm acting like this—I think I'm just worried about him. And if I'm honest, I don't like the idea of him going out with Oskar.

"What time do you think you'll be back?" I ask quietly.

"I know Mum has probably told you to look out for me, but I'll be okay. I have been out at night before, you know. I am eighteen." He gives me a smile—he's trying to reassure me.

He looks so high and happy, and I feel so awful for feeling how I'm feeling. I'm scared my unhappiness will bleed through me into him.

"You don't really know Oskar, though."

"That's why I'm going out with him."

Feeling sick, I follow him to the front door. There is a taxi waiting in the road.

Angus checks his wallet and his phone, and then turns to me.

"I just want to go out, have a friend. I want to know what it's like. What are you worried about, Josh?"

"I don't know," I say honestly.

I want to follow him outside, but I don't. Instead I stand in the doorway, rubbing my bare arms with my hands. Watching as Angus gets in the taxi, and it drives away down the road.

IT'S HALF one when I hear a car pull up outside. I can hear someone stumbling up the path and fumbling with the lock on the communal front door.

By the time I'm downstairs, Angus has managed to open the front door, but he's not managed to get any further than that. Instead he's slumped on the threshold half-asleep.

"Angus?" I kneel down beside him.

He groans, but when he doesn't respond further, I hoist him into my arms and help him upright. He's solid and heavy, and for someone who never seems to do any exercise other than running, he has a lot of muscle under those clothes. There is not an ounce of fat on him. If I ran like he does, I'd just get leaner. I wouldn't bulk up like this. My hand fastens around his waist. I try and flatten it out, though I desperately want to trace the contours of the muscles I can feel. But I will not grope him when he is drunk and half-aware. I roll my eyes. *I will not grope him anyway!*

With Angus staggering against me, we make it to his flat. I still have the spare key, and propping him up against the wall, my hand against his chest to stop him sliding down it like I know he wants to, I unlock the door.

Inside the flat, it is a tip. Angus is really not the tidiest person to have ever walked the earth, and with no one to encourage him to be tidier, the flat has just degraded into a mess. Textbooks and notes are strewn across the floor, a stack of dirty plates sits on the work surface, and there are half-finished mugs of tea *everywhere*. No wonder he keeps coming upstairs to me to watch TV and eat.

With my free hand, I flick the light switch—I don't want to stand on anything that's not made for being stood on—and half carry Angus in with me. He winces, holding his hand over his eyes. We make it as far as the sofa. I reason it's far enough and let him flop down.

"Turn the light off," he groans, curling onto his side away from me.

"What's the magic word?"

"*Josh*," he whines.

Well, at least he's sentient enough to know who I am.

"How was your date?" I ask, reaching to switch on the floor lamp next to the sofa and then walking back into the hall to turn off the overhead light.

Angus grumbles something. I lean down to hear him better.

"Sleep," he moans. Then "Come 'ere."

Flinging his arm out, he catches me around the shoulder and tugs me closer. He smells of alcohol, smoke, and cold winter air, and something other—some scent that seeps under my skin and makes me want to press closer. For a moment I can't do anything but breathe him in, my cheek pressed to his hair.

"You waited up for me, didn't you?" he half mumbles. His eyes are closed, but his lips curve in a lazy smile. "Though you'd never admit it."

I hate that sometimes it seems as if he can read my mind. He's never been this direct with me before.

"You're deluded," I whisper.

"Probably," he agrees.

He turns his head and his cheek presses against mine. I try to ignore the way my cock is stiffening, but my arousal is quickly becoming full-blown.

For minutes we don't move. A battle is raging inside me, rendering me immobile.

I don't remember putting my arm around him. I only notice when Angus groans and shivers as my fingers stroke the small patch of bare skin on his stomach where his T-shirt has ridden up. The soft dark hair there feels silky to my touch. I can see his thick erection straining the tight fabric of his jeans, a bare inch from my fingertips. I want to touch it so badly, I'm trembling—blood is pounding in my ears.

"When Oskar kissed me, I thought about you," he breathes hotly into my ear. He arches his back and pushes his hips up, causing his T-shirt to ride up farther. "I didn't let him suck me off. I wanted to come home and take my clothes off and think about you some more."

The thought of Oskar kissing him makes me feel hollow and hurting. I pull away.

"Don't," I mutter, closing my eyes.

When I open them, Angus is staring at me—the black of his pupils swallowing up the gray of his irises.

"Be with me. Just once," he says. Suddenly he seems as sober as anything—whereas I feel as drunk as all hell on his proximity, his warmth, his sweetness. "Just one night, and then we can go back to being friends, or whatever you want."

"It doesn't work like that."

"You're as turned-on as I am."

I don't even try to shift and hide the erection he can see tenting my sweatpants. I'm so hard it hurts not to be pressed up against him, my cock longing for his warmth. And I can no longer deny that it's him my body wants.

"That doesn't mean it would be a good idea," I say tightly, suddenly angry at Angus for pushing me and angry at myself for letting him.

"I don't *want* anyone else." The raw emotion in his voice and his expression terrifies me.

"You're drunk, Angus." I use every single ounce of willpower I have ever possessed to push myself up off the floor. "I'm going to bed. I'll come and check on you in the morning."

Walking away from him hurts like fuck. It's as though there is a magnetic pull between our bodies. My dick is aching for him so badly. And it's not just my dick. Something in my chest is pulled so fucking taut.

Chapter 6

A QUIET knock on my door wakes me. Blurry-eyed, I blink at my phone, waiting for the numbers to stop dancing around so I can read the time. It's half past four, and I feel terrible. A light sheen of sweat coats my skin. I'm not awake enough to wonder why someone is knocking on my door—when no one ever knocks on my door—at half past four in the morning.

Unless it's an emergency.

Scrubbing my face with my hands, I get up, grab a pair of tracksuit bottoms off the floor, pull them up my naked body, and hurry to the front door.

Angus is standing outside, looking awkward and upset. He pulls at the frayed hem of his black hooded sweatshirt, and I wonder if he sleeps in those heavy-looking clothes, because he must be boiling if he does.

Since there seems to be no immediate panic, my first thought is that he's freaking out again and missing Eleanor. But he's never appeared at my door in the middle of the night before, and she's been gone over a week now. He's not a kid—however hard it is for me to accept that sometimes.

"You okay?" I ask, still squinting at the brightness of the lights, my head throbbing so hard it's as if someone is whacking a rock against my skull.

"Can I come in?"

"Of course."

Trying not to move too quickly because of the pain in my head, I step back and open the door wide.

It's funny that a few short weeks ago, no one had been in my flat, and now Angus strides inside like it's his second home. He hesitates in the hallway, seeming undecided about which room to head for—not that there is much choice in my small flat—it's either the living room or the kitchen. After a heartbeat Angus decides on the kitchen.

"I saw someone at the window," he says tensely, gripping the edge of my tiny kitchen table.

"What?"

"I woke up to pee, and I saw a shadow through the curtains in Mum's room."

I smile at his word choice, though I quickly let it drop away when I notice the reproachful look he's giving me. Under the harsh kitchen lights, Angus's skin looks wan and sickly pale, as though he's ill and all of his usual brightness has fled. Dark shadows make his eyes appear large and haunted.

"I feel like crap," he moans, making me think perhaps we do have some sort of telepathic connection. Shakily he brings his hand up to his head.

"Funnily enough, alcohol does that," I say, moving past him to get a packet of paracetamol out of the cabinet in the bathroom. Filling a glass with water, I hand it to him with the tablets, swallowing a couple down myself before I put the packet away. "It's mostly dehydration that makes you feel like crap."

I resist the urge to lecture him. I've never known him to go out and get wasted like that before. Perhaps it was his first time.

He swallows the tablets and downs the rest of the water.

"There was someone outside, Josh. Just standing there.... Definitely a person this time."

"Okay. I'll go take a look," I say reluctantly.

It's not that I don't believe him, it's just I know what it's like when you're on your own and someone has planted the seed of an idea. Paranoia gathers momentum—a snowball of fear that builds and builds as it rolls round your mind. All sorts of shapes can come to life in the dark and quiet of the night.

"No," he says, wincing as he shakes his head.

I raise my eyebrows.

"I don't...." He swallows. "If there is someone there... I don't want you to get hurt."

It's been so long since anyone has worried about me like this, it makes me weak inside. And even though I feel awful, the bone-deep want I feel in his presence is just getting stronger and harder to ignore.

I KEEP a heavy torch under my bed. It's shaped a bit like a cosh. My own paranoia had me buying it many years ago now for self-defense.

As he's followed me into the bedroom, I show it to Angus with a flourish and a tired grin.

"Protection and a torch all in one," I say.

I try not to look round the bedroom. I'm embarrassed by the dirty clothes I discarded last night on the floor, the way my bed looks as though I've been wrestling with a fucking octopus in it. Normally, no one else sees in here. The rest of the flat is immaculate. I like order. But if Angus notices, he doesn't give any indication.

"I'm coming with you," he says.

He still looks far too fearful.

I roll my eyes in mock exasperation, even though doing so feels like my eyeballs are moving against ground-up glass. "Come on, then."

OUR TEETH are chattering, and we're shivering even before we've stepped off the porch. A deep breathy hush of icy morning air surrounds us, and for a moment we stop, just listening, just breathing. Being outside right now, searching for some phantom that isn't here, is the last thing I want to be doing. I want to be in bed, sleeping off this headache that's making my vision blur.

After a moment's hesitation, I grab Angus's hand and lead him across the frozen grass and around the side of the building. I don't pull out the torch until the streetlights no longer reach us and even our tightly joined hands are swallowed up by the gloom.

"Which window?" I breathe.

Angus freezes by my side until I switch the torch on and point it at him. He looks terrified, and I'm beginning to lose circulation in the hand he's squeezing the life out of.

I'm just about one hundred percent certain there is no one here.

Giving his hand a good squeeze of my own, I pull him after me as we make a circuit of the house—all the way round the back and down the side alley, with me flicking my torch up and down and around and around as though I'm trying to bring down planes out of the sky.

No one.

I don't ask Angus if he's happy now we've checked everywhere—I can see that he's not.

Upstairs, Angus sits with his head rested on his arms at my tiny kitchen table while I make him a hot chocolate. I think about pouring a small measure of brandy in it to help him sleep, but he's already had too much alcohol tonight.

"Can I sleep up here tonight?" he asks, looking so fucking unsure of whether or not I'm going to say yes.

"There's not much night left, you know." It's nearly half five, but it's Sunday, and I'm not working.

"I'm sorry I woke you up, and I'm sorry about coming on to you earlier."

He won't meet my gaze. I can hear his foot tapping against the floor.

"Wasn't sure you'd remember. You seemed really out of it." I try to sound offhand, wanting him to know we can forget it.

"Not that out of it."

Obviously.

"Come on, I'll let you have the bed," I say. *Because I just love sleeping on the sofa.*

In the bedroom I pick up my mess of clothes off the floor, then sit with him while he finishes his drink.

I move to get up, but Angus hesitantly touches my hand. "Stay here with me. I promise I won't come on to you again or anything. I just want to be near someone."

"I'll only be in the next room."

"Please, Josh," he whispers. "I feel so fucking awful. Not just hungover. I feel so fucking lonely and scared."

It's his expression rather than his words that make me stay. He looks so utterly vulnerable and exposed, it actually hurts me. I try and clamp down on the feeling, but I can't, and I know the only thing that's going to help is being close to him.

I turn out the light and scoot into bed behind him, pulling him into my arms so we're spooned together tightly, my hands against his heart. It feels so wonderful, and I know I can never, ever let this happen again. Not if I want to hold myself together. Not if I want to keep a grip on my life. I don't want to be on the front of this train when it crashes and burns.

"Hangovers are the worst," I whisper, his ear barely a millimeter from my lips. "They can make everything seem so bad."

"It feels so good when you hold me, though." He brings his hands up to cover mine, squeezing our fingers together gently.

I move my hands away. He promised me he wouldn't do this.

"Don't," I say gently, smoothing his hair with my fingertips.

His chest trembles, and I hear him sob. The sounds he makes are just tiny gasps, as if he's trying desperately to hold it all inside. I pull him closer because I don't know what else to do. I feel closer to him than I've felt to anyone in a long, long time.

However much he's hurting, it's not long before Angus is asleep. I watch him in the half darkness, my hands splayed out protectively across his chest, feeling his heart beat against my fingers. I should get up and go lie down in the other room, I should snap all these threads that I can feel wrapping around us tighter and tighter, because Angus deserves so much better than what I can offer him. He deserves someone who is not so fucked-up and afraid. He deserves someone who will love him and be there for him until the end of the fucking world. He doesn't deserve another burden, another broken person in his life.

But I can't snap the threads, and I can't move away.

However much I tell myself there are no triggers for my depression that I can't deal with, I know there is one, and this is it. Feeling like this. Wanting a normality I know is out of my reach. Wishing there was a way I could fix the faulty wiring in my brain. Wishing I could promise to never hurt him.

Angus smells like heaven, and I'm lost, so lost. My throat feels tight, and I squeeze my eyes shut.

Eventually I sleep.

WHEN I wake, Angus is gone.

My first thought is it's a bit strange that I didn't wake when he left—I'm such a light sleeper usually—but perhaps it's because I don't feel so good. I try and raise my head, but it feels heavy, and the slightest movement causes me pain.

Forcing myself upright, I have to wait for the room to stop spinning before I get up and gingerly change my clothes. I can't face a shower even though I'm covered in sweat again and my stomach is roiling like an unstill sea. I ignore it as best I can.

For a while I wander restlessly from room to room. When I can wait no more, I go downstairs to knock on Angus's door.

I don't know what it is exactly, but something changed last night, and I just want to see him. It's probably quite pathetic, especially as I feel so ill I'm actually shaking and ready to curl up on the cold hard tiles beneath my feet.

The door opens.

"Oh," Angus says when he sees me. His gaze flicks away from my face almost immediately.

He doesn't seem unwelcoming exactly, just a little closed off, and I can't remember him ever being closed off with me before.

"How are you feeling?" Even my voice sounds tight and sick.

"Pretty crap," he answers, and I get the sense he means more than physically, though it's hard to tell when he's barely even looked at me. "I've got some studying to do."

"Want to come up?"

Even though I'm not feeling one hundred percent, I still want his company. I guess that should tell me something, but it's just not something I'm willing to consciously accept right now.

He shakes his head, continuing to look down at the tiles.

"Is everything okay?"

"Fine," he says tightly.

This conversation is making me grit my teeth a little.

"I should get back to work." He moves to shut the door.

"Wait." I put my arm on the door to stop it closing. "Is this something to do with last night? Is something else worrying you?"

Angus sags against the doorframe. "I wish you weren't so nice to me. Sometimes I wish you were just my upstairs neighbor. Someone I could go and borrow some sugar from and crush on in secret, knowing nothing would ever happen between us, but that would be okay, because that's what secret crushes are for," he whispers.

"What?" I'm genuinely perplexed.

"You've no idea what this is doing to me, do you?" For a second his gaze flashes against mine, his eyes full of so much pain.

I open my mouth and close it again, swallowing whatever words I was going to say, because maybe he's right—I don't know.

I step backwards until my hands touch the cool wall behind me. I need something to hold on to, something to hold my shaky body upright.

"Maybe it would be better if we don't bump into each other at all for a while. Please don't go and see Mum straight after you've finished work. Go later in the evening, and I'll make sure I'm not there."

He closes the door to his flat.

I stare at the dark wood, feeling light-headed.

Somehow I make it upstairs. My head is spinning, my stomach cramping painfully. I just make it to the toilet before throwing up—retching and retching until my stomach is empty and it's mostly bile. After, my legs feel so weak I can't stand, and I curl up on the floor. I wonder if I have food poisoning and think back over what I ate last night, but it was nothing out of the ordinary.

From where I'm lying, I can just about see the galaxies pasted on the ceiling. The stars bursting and full of light, the cold stark emptiness that surrounds them.

I DON'T go to work on Monday. I still feel awful. I can't even remember if I phoned in sick. Somehow I managed to crawl from the bathroom and into bed last night, and now I can't get out of it. I just can't move. It's as though a heavy weight is pinning me in place. My body wants to throw up, but I have nothing left, and I just retch into the sorry towel by my bedside.

Sometime in the evening, there is a knock at my door, but I don't answer it or even call out. I don't have enough energy.

I'm not sure if I sleep or not. There are just huge blank spaces of time where I do nothing at all.

It might be Tuesday when I hear Soren's unmistakable voice. He knocks loudly on my door and calls my name.

But he goes away again.

It's dark when I hear a key being turned in the lock. I think I must be dreaming. Eleanor has a key to my flat. I got it cut for her years ago, but she's never used it. Maybe she's come up to see if I'm okay. It takes a moment for me to remember she's not here anymore.

I open my eyes, and two people are standing in my room talking. Someone is sitting on my bed. It's Angus. He's touching my wrist. At first I think he's just holding it, but then I notice he's taking my pulse. He places his hand against my forehead and looks at me solemnly. Soren is with him, holding a tray of food. He puts the tray on the floor when he sees my eyes are open.

I think I hear Emma's voice somewhere in the vicinity of my kitchen.

"Josh, can you sit up?"

Slipping his arms around me, Angus helps me. He looks awful—haunted. He hands me a glass of water.

God, I'm thirsty. My throat is so dry, it feels swollen. I don't think I could speak even if I wanted to.

"Josh, what the fuck is going on?" Soren says abruptly, pacing back and forth across my room. "I thought you were fucking dying or something…! Are you dying or something?" he adds worriedly.

I've never heard Soren sound worried before.

Angus shoots him a warning glance and mutters something like, "Don't," under his breath.

I'm not sure I can speak.

"All right, all right, I'll come back in a minute," Soren says, waving his arms in the air and disappearing into the kitchen.

I don't really understand why everyone is in my flat.

"Did you just suddenly come down with something? What happened?" Angus asks once Soren is gone.

He scoots closer. The glass is so heavy in my hands, I think I might drop it. Angus notices and helps me bring it up to my mouth. His hands are warm, strong.

"Tired," I whisper after I've taken a sip.

"Soren told me you haven't been in to work for two days. Not even called in sick or anything. I thought you were just keeping out of my way like I'd asked. I was so worried about you when Soren told me."

"Don't worry."

Angus sits with me. Makes me eat the soup Soren brought in on the tray. Surprisingly I find I'm hungry, and I eat the lot. I feel a little better. A little more alive, less pinned in place. When Soren comes back in, Angus takes the tray away and leaves us.

I think I can hear Emma talking on her phone, or maybe she's talking to Angus in the kitchen about the porn. Poor shy Angus.

"So are you still sick? Should we call a doctor?"

I shake my head, which isn't actually hurting. Now it just feels full of low-grade static and echoes.

"Then you need to get up and get on, and not lie there and wallow."

Wallow? Do I look like I'm wallowing?

"You need to work on your bedside manner," I mutter.

Soren raises an eyebrow. "You've no idea what my bedside manner is like."

"I'm serious, Soren. I don't need all this fuss, everyone here." I pull a pained face. I'm not in the mood for his teasing or games. I feel so weak.

"If you suddenly just drop off the radar and don't turn up for work or call in sick or *anything*, and you make everyone who cares about you worry, then you're going to get a fuss." Soren folds his arms across his chest.

"I still feel like crap, all right. Leave me alone."

Soren shrugs, his face like stone. "You look well enough to get up. You can stay in here as long as you want, but I'm not leaving your flat until you can get out of that bed and I know you're okay."

He really is a pain in the arse.

"And anyway, I quite like reading the walls in your kitchen," he calls over his shoulder as he stalks out.

I can hear them all talking. I close my eyes and try to shut them out. When I open my eyes again, Angus is leaning against the doorframe, watching me. He brushes his hair out of his eyes and smiles, though it's not a happy smile. I get the sense that he's been upset, but I'm not sure how I know that. He looks pale, but maybe it's just because of his dark clothes, because he's not pale. Even in winter he glows a warm shade of gold.

"I'm going to see Mum in a bit, but I can come up and check on you later… if you like?" As he speaks, he fiddles with the leather strap wrapped round his wrist.

"Can you get rid of Soren?" I groan.

Angus smiles wryly. “I doubt it.” But his smile quickly fades, and we stare at each other, though this time I look away first. “What I said the other day… I didn’t mean it. Any of it. I hate not seeing you. Can we go back to how things were before?” he asks quietly.

“Okay.”

It might not show on my face, but inside I’m smiling, and some part of me that’s higher than my stomach but lower than my heart is doing little flips of joy.

He may as well have his hand around my heart.

Chapter 7

EVENTUALLY I get up.

Emma and Soren fuss around making sure I've got everything I need and watching me as though they suspect I might collapse to the floor at any moment. When they're gone I begrudgingly admit Soren was right to make me get out of bed. I shower and dress, and I'm surprised to find I'm okay. Exhausted, but okay.

It's a relief, because however much I convince myself I *was* actually just sick, underneath it all I was terrified the last few days were a lapse back into the darkness that paralyzed me before. I was terrified that the abyss had opened up inside me again, that my depression had come to swallow me.

But I didn't fall apart. I'm not falling apart.

As I butter myself slice after slice of toast to make up for the last two days' lack of food, I think perhaps I'm stronger than I thought. I think perhaps I won't slip back under so easily.

IT'S DUSK and I'm sitting in the window seat when I see Angus walking back from the hospital carrying a bag of shopping. His head is down and his free hand is in his pocket as he kicks at the rubbish that litters the pavement, the bag swinging against his leg. A car passes, and he looks up, not at the car but right up toward my window. The light is so low I'm not sure he sees me, but I experience a pleasure so intense I don't think I could ever articulate it. My world has shifted. Something that I thought was broken is flickering to life inside me, fixing itself and filling me with so much energy, I don't quite know what to do with it. I put my book down and get up to go downstairs and meet him.

His eyes light up, and he grins when he sees me waiting. Surprised, I think.

"You're feeling better," he says, closing the communal front door behind him, his gaze checking me over.

I nod. "Much. Just wrung out. How's Eleanor?"

"Anxious. She's worried about you. About not seeing you. I had to lie. Told her they needed you to do extra shifts at work. I hate lying, but I was scared she'd only worry more if she knew you were sick."

"I'm sorry you had to lie."

Some people lie with such ease, it's as though it's part of their personality, but others are just so straightforward and true that lying cuts them deep.

Angus shrugs. "I brought you some food." He holds out the bag of shopping, biting his lip and blushing so hard I can almost feel the heat of it. "Are you busy…? I could…."

"Come upstairs?" I finish for him. I give him a lopsided smile. A smile he returns a hundredfold.

In my kitchen I smile at him gratefully as I unpack the food he bought me and make some more toast.

"Hungry," I explain. "Want something?"

Angus shakes his head. "I should do a bit of studying."

"Want to do it up here?"

"Okay."

I catch him still staring at me as I shove toast into my mouth, and I slow down a bit—I don't want to look like I'm stuffing my face (even though I am).

"It's complicated, isn't it, this…." He frowns at his hand before looking up again. "Whatever it is… between us?"

I stop chewing my mouthful of toast. Angus keeps looking at me steadily, but his chest is rising and falling more quickly than it was a moment ago as he waits for my reaction.

I barely move my head, yet Angus's relief at my response is palpable.

"It's okay. Complicated is okay," he says brightly, before getting up to go and retrieve his textbooks from downstairs.

I stare after him, my toast growing cold in my hand, knowing without a doubt that this thing between us is not complicated. What's complicated is me. Angus is as uncomplicated and true as an arrow shot right through my heart.

THE NEXT day I feel much better. I phone Soren and tell him I'm coming into work—he'd signed me off for the rest of the week, but his comments about getting up and getting on stirred something inside me. And mostly I'm tired but not at all sick anymore.

As I leave, I debate knocking on Angus's door, but I have no idea whether he will be awake, whether he is a morning person or not, so I leave it. This complicated thing between us feels so fragile now, and I'm scared of breaking it.

I stride out the front door and almost trip over Oskar, who is sitting topless on the doorstep outside, smoking. His still plastered foot is stuck out in front of him, his ragged jeans rolled up above it.

We stare at each other, the both of us wide-eyed with shock.

"Hi," Oskar says after a heartbeat.

I think my mouth may be open, but no sound comes out. I can't stop staring at his pale skinny chest as my brain fills in the gaps as to why he has no top on. Why he's here outside the house in the first place, freezing his nipples off. He must have spent the night with Angus and is smoking out here because Angus knows Eleanor wouldn't want anyone smoking in her flat. My stomach lurches, and the newly wired hope around my heart short-circuits in my chest.

"Angus," I say, without really knowing why. I have nothing to follow it with.

Oskar nods.

"I've got to go to work now," I mumble, turning quickly and walking away.

My journey to work is a blur.

My brain has gone into overdrive. Self-loathing is a bitch always looking for her chance. And I know I'm being melodramatic and jumping to conclusions, but maybe it'd be for the best if Angus fell in love with Oskar. Perhaps Oskar can give Angus what I can't. Actually, I'm pretty sure he can. So why does the thought of them together make me feel like I'm collapsing inside? Why do I keep thinking back to how Angus looked at me yesterday when he asked me if it was complicated? Why does being with him make me feel so fucking hopeful and alive?

Feeling so much is what terrifies me. Feeling so much and not being able to make any sense of it.

This is why you have to keep your distance, I remind myself bitterly. *Don't feel, don't ever let anyone reach beneath the surface and your world will stay intact and not crumble around your feet.*

"Are you going to make me regret thinking you were okay enough to work?" Soren says with a frown when he sees me waiting for him to open up by the front of the shop.

Today he's wearing the hat with the earflaps he wears when it's cold. *The deerstalker.* Not everyone can pull off the dorky earflap hat, but with his high cheekbones, angular jaw, and unusual coloring, he looks like a poster boy for some hip winter-clothing line. Well, that or a Sherlock Holmes wannabe.

"I *am* okay to work," I assure him, smiling tightly.

"God, that's scary. Please don't do it again," he says dryly.

I actually laugh—not knowing how that is possible when I'm the closest to crying I've come in years.

Stupid thing about crying is when you *think* about doing it, you sometimes find yourself *actually* doing it.

"Shit." Soren grabs my arm and pulls me inside the shop. In a second he has an arm around my shoulder, pulling me into an awkward embrace, overwhelming me with his aftershave and his kindness.

Mortified, I shove him away and wipe my eyes. I can't believe I've done this in front of him.

"I'm okay," I say again, determined to keep the tremor out of my voice.

"No, you're not."

"Shit, Soren, that's not helping, okay.... Just... just give me a minute."

Holding up his hands, he steps away and flicks the shop lights on.

"I'm making you a sugary coffee, and you're going to drink it, and afterwards, if you still look like you're going to frighten children, you're going home."

I MANAGE to annoy Soren into letting me stay at work. I don't want to go home. In fact I am dreading going home. My head is a mess. At least here I can pretend everything is normal and okay.

"So, I take it you've not made a move on that neighbor of yours?"

Soren stands next to me at the cash register filling out an invoice.

"What neighbor?"

"Pretending you don't know what the fuck I'm talking about doesn't actually work when I've been in the same room as you two," he says, shaking his head and looking at me as though he cannot believe I'm denying this.

"What's that supposed to mean?"

"That I think you want him, and when he looks at you, he just about melts. I'm betting he will do absolutely anything you ask him to—which, by the way, is kinda hot. *Waaay* hot, actually. And yet, here you are, still as sexually frustrated as ever." He sighs, smiling innocently.

"I don't want him," I say stubbornly, glowering. *And I am not sexually frustrated!* I want to shout.

Soren is really starting to piss me off.

I SPEND the rest of the day avoiding the raised eyebrows and suggestive little smirks Soren gives me whenever he glances my way. He knows he's fucking right, and I hate his smugness.

"DON'T COME in tomorrow. I'll get Emma to cover for you—she needs the hours," Soren says as we're closing up.

“What? Why not?” I lock the front of the shop, feeling a sharp spike of panic at this suggestion. Is he thinking about cutting my hours permanently? It’s well within his role as shop manager to do that.

“Take the day off. Do something fun. Go to the seaside—take Angus. Have a picnic. Anything. Get it out of your system.”

“You’re giving me the day off to go hook up with someone?” I raise my eyebrows incredulously.

“No, I’m giving you the day off to go sort yourself out.” Pulling down the shutter, Soren sighs as if he thinks he really shouldn’t have to be telling me this. “Ever since that burglary, you’ve been a mess. And now I know why. It’s all connected to Angus. Figure it out, Josh. Don’t be a dick about it.”

Soren is the last person I’m willing to accept advice from, and yet, perhaps he’s right. Perhaps I do need to sort myself out. Perhaps I should get in my car and just drive, just put my foot down and keep going. I don’t even think about where Angus fits into all this. I no longer have to—my heart just knows. But now everything is unraveled and out of my control. I’ve held back for too long.

ANGUS IS waiting in the hall as usual when I get home. He smiles when he sees me, lit up with happiness. *It’s probably Oskar’s presence*, I think despondently.

“Hey,” I say. I go for upbeat, but it comes out flat.

Even though I’ve convinced myself he’d be happier with Oskar, trying to mask the wave of hurt I feel is harder than I thought.

“Finished my studying, so we could… I could—” Looking incredibly self-conscious, he swallows and shifts from foot to foot. His hands are behind his back as though he’s hiding something. “—cook something for you if you like?” He produces a recipe and what looks to be a small plastic bag of ingredients.

“I’m tired,” I mutter, hating myself.

I walk past him and up the stairs.

"Oskar said he saw you this morning," Angus says quickly, taking the stairs two at a time and following me. "He's staying with me for a bit. He was supposed to be staying with a friend, but it fell through."

I reach my door.

"We're just friends," Angus says.

I stop. He thinks I'm jealous, and I am, but not in the way he thinks.

"It's okay," I say quietly, just wanting to get inside my flat and shut the door.

"Jesus, Josh. Can you just… look at me?"

I turn.

"I'm not fucking interested in Oskar. Okay?" He sounds exasperated. "I'd have thought you'd be able to work that out by now."

It's more Angus swearing that has me paying attention than anything else. Angus hardly ever swears. That and the look on his face that tells me… well, it tells me whatever he's feeling right now, he doesn't feel that way about Oskar.

It'd be so easy to lose myself in his eyes, in the intensity of his gaze. *Please give me a chance*, he seems to be begging me, and I want to. Oh God, I want to. I want to give us a chance more than anything.

I want to trust him.

"I want to cook you something. I owe you. *Please*?" he says.

My resistance has evaporated.

Holding my door wide, I let him in.

"I'M GOING to take a shower," I say as Angus peers around the kitchen looking for pans and knives and a chopping board. He nods distractedly, smoothing out the recipe sheet on the small kitchen table and staring at it.

"Can I ask what you're cooking?"

I try and glance past him at what's been handwritten on the sheet, but he steps in front of it so I can't see.

"It's a surprise," he says, his blush deepening the longer we look at each other.

I shrug, smiling a little, the weight in my chest lightening as though I'm being slowly filled with helium. *Okay.*

I take my time, standing under the shower far longer than normal, the warm spray washing over me. In my stomach it feels as though I have swallowed one of those tiny bouncy rubber balls and it's just bouncing around inside me. The sensation increases as I pass the kitchen and see Angus concentrating as he chops something and scrapes it into the pan. It smells wonderful, and I just want to lean against the doorjamb and watch him. Even if watching him is turning me on.

In the bedroom I have a bit of a clothing crisis, thinking jogging bottoms and the T-shirt I slept in are somehow not appropriate, but not really knowing what is. I don't know why I'm so nervous either. I've eaten meals with Angus plenty of times now.

As soon as I step into the kitchen, Angus hands me a beer and gestures for me to sit down. The lights are off, and the room is full of candlelight. Bright little tea lights cover all the work surfaces and are dotted across the table. He must have found them in one of the drawers.

"I can turn the lights back on if it's a bit weird," Angus says hesitantly as I stare around. "Or… or if you think it's a fire hazard or something."

"No, it's okay." My hands are shaking as I pick at the label on the beer bottle in my hands.

Angus carefully places a piled-up plate in front of me. It's a warm bacon and potato salad with warm crusty bread croutons—simple fare, but effective enough to bring a pressure behind my eyes that I have to blink away.

"No one has ever cooked for me like this before. Thank you," I say, wondering where this desire to be so open has come from. It's not as if I'm about to tell Angus about the lack of friends or lovers in my life, but I'm aware I'm hinting at it.

"Thank you for letting me," Angus says, sitting down opposite. His eyes appear so dark in this light. His cheek dimples as he tries not to smile.

We don't speak much, but it's okay. It's not necessary. Afterwards Angus washes up and makes coffee, and we sit in the living room, our thighs pressed together on the velvet couch. His hands flutter in his lap as if he wants to do something with them but is unsure what, and he fiddles with the strap around his wrist. I think about holding his hand, but I don't. I wonder if that's what he wants me to do.

Slowly he relaxes. He laughs at a few stupid jokes I tell him. I discover I have a talent for a simple sort of humor, or maybe Angus just finds everything I say funny. I don't know. But we grow silent after a while. He leans his head against my shoulder, and I just breathe him in. The sweetness of these moments becomes too perfect to spoil with too many words. I am so content just *being* with him. I want to share my silence with him. I've never felt like this with anyone before. It's as if some subatomic shift is taking place inside me. The change is so fundamental, it worries me that a part of my brain has still not recovered from my being sick.

When Angus tells me he should go home, I don't want him to.

"You need to rest," he says gently and gets up.

"Stay," I say softly. I hold his gaze, trying, for once, to impart my own meaning in our secret shared connection.

"Another time," he says but he looks as though he has to force the words out.

I walk him to the front door, pulling him into my arms before either of us feels awkward about what we're supposed to do now, how we're supposed to say good-bye. We hold each other like that for a long time, my nose pressing into his hair, his soft lips on my collarbone. Angus's heart thumps against my chest. I love how warm and excited he feels. My whole body is thrumming and stiff with excitement for *him*. I want to kiss him, but he told me he wants to go, so instead I move my head and whisper in his ear, "Are you free tomorrow?"

"Yeah, I can be. What for?" His voice is just muffled breath against my neck, but it feels wonderful.

"Want to come to the beach with me?"

"Yes."

I can hear the smile in his voice, feel it against my skin.

Chapter 8

WE LEAVE early, heading down south toward Brighton. Although I have no intention of actually going to Brighton, the beaches on the south coast are the best (and the nearest).

It promises to be a beautiful day, though Angus and I do have to scrape ice off the car windscreen before we set off, and I turn the heater up to full sunshine hot. But beauty is relative, and we could be going anywhere and doing anything and it would be nothing less.

Angus dozes off in the passenger seat for the first hour. He looks exhausted and maybe a little stressed. There are dark rings under his eyes. I wonder if he's pushing himself too hard over this test for college.

The test is the day after tomorrow. I didn't want him worrying about it, so I asked him before we left if he wanted to bring any textbooks along, but he stopped himself and told me he's studied enough and a little revision later will be fine. I know he wants so badly to do well, but it's not worth putting himself under so much pressure. I don't think he should have to. Not that I would ever tell him for fear of sounding like a patronizing parent, but I'm so proud of him.

AT AROUND half eight I pull over for a cup of tea at a breakfast van in a lay-by right at the top of the South Downs. Angus climbs out of the car, yawning and stretching as though he needs a few more hours in bed. His T-shirt rides up, and I stare at the neatly defined line of jet-black hair that descends his flat stomach, disappearing below the waistband of his jeans. He catches my eye, and I quickly look away across the frosty Downs, everything glittering in the hazy morning sunlight.

"It's pretty up here," Angus says.

We lean against the car, drinking our tea and taking in the view. A couple of other cars are parked up with people doing the same thing. I can feel the heat of Angus's body even though we're half a foot apart.

"I made you breakfast," I say. "Do you want it now or when we get to the beach?"

"The beach." He smiles. "I've never seen the sea."

"Really?" I admit I'm a little shocked. On this small island, surely everyone has been to the seaside by the time they're eighteen. But perhaps even before she stopped going out of the house, Eleanor didn't like going too far away. And by the sounds of it, Angus's shit of a father has never done anything just for Angus.

There is a beautiful emptyish expanse of beach near the garish seaside resort of Hayling Island. I park up and for a moment let Angus just stare out the windscreen as I go and buy a day's parking ticket. In the distance there are a few dogs racing across the sand, their walkers slowly ambling behind them. Apart from them, we are mostly alone.

The sea is so far out, the beach looks as though it might stretch right up to the horizon. Almost. If it weren't for the flickering, sea-glass glint of light as it glances blindingly from distant wave to distant wave, I might think the beach goes on forever.

Out of the car boot, I pick up the picnic blanket and the rucksack full of food I prepared this morning, and we set off across the stones toward the never ending stretch of sand. But the wind is so bitterly cold, we head back inland after a couple of minutes to find a little shelter amongst the sand dunes to eat our breakfast. I even wish for a couple of Soren's god-awful silly hats to protect us from the icy breeze.

Angus's enthusiasm is undimmed. He grins at me when I hand him a bacon roll.

"You're amazing, you do know that, right?" he says, taking a bite. The wind whips his hair in front of his face.

I raise one eyebrow, pretending I'm cooler than the freezing December air, but I think by now Angus gets it that I'm not all that cool beneath the surface. I don't know how exactly, but I think perhaps he's always seen behind the front I put up. Maybe I'm just writing on a wall to him. I'm not sure how I feel about that—elated, terrified, embarrassed, relieved. I'm a secret that has never been told. Maybe we all are until someone cracks our code.

Perhaps I shouldn't analyze.

"I hoped it wasn't going to be quite so cold and windy." I sigh.

"It's exhilarating! We should go swimming." He gestures excitedly at the too distant freezing sea.

I roll my eyes, but half an hour later, I'm standing barefoot in the sand, my shoes in my hand, the achingly cold water lapping against my ankles. *This is what going for a walk with an overgrown puppy must be like*, I think wryly.

Angus wades a little deeper, gesturing that I follow him. With the wind blowing in his hair, he looks so wildly beautiful and free it makes my stomach do the mad little flip thing it's started to do whenever I am around him. Just being near him makes me feel exhilarated. My breath is whipped away by the sea.

What can I do but walk into the sea after him?

THERE ARE few stones and shells in the sand but Angus digs out what he can find as souvenirs. I'm mesmerized by him, by the expressions of wonderment he tries to hide. Glancing up, he attempts to hold himself in check, but he can't. He's far too open, and I never want him to be anything else.

"I'm being too much a kid, aren't I?"

"No. Never." I shake my head with a smile.

Standing up, he pouts. He looks as if he's about to say something else, but as he steps backwards, his face twists in pain. I reach out to grab him, but I'm not fast enough, and he collapses down onto the sand, gripping his foot.

Shocked, I drop the shoes I'm carrying and sink down on the sand next to him.

"What happened?"

Angus's only response is a sort of strangled gasp as he pulls a thin piece of clear glass out of his heel and blood begins to gush everywhere over the wet sand.

Oh shit.

"We need to get you back to the car," I say, trying to keep it calm and together even though I can feel how hard I'm shaking.

I pick up the shoes and slip my arm around his back to help him to his feet.

"I'm okay," he says.

Wincing, he tries to hop. *It's going to take forever to get to the car like this.*

I give him the shoes to hold, and I lift him into my arms. Although he's shorter than me, he's broader, and his leanness is all muscle. It's a long way back across the sand, and I am still exhausted from how sick I was earlier in the week. My arms are aching in protest, but I don't even register the discomfort fully.

Angus makes no protest to being carried. Instead he grips his hands around my neck and presses close. If I weren't so worried, it would be a turn-on.

Blood drips from his cut heel, leaving a thin red ribbon that trails behind us.

"You're losing too much blood." I stumble painfully across the stones to the car. I'm ready to bundle him up and put my foot to the floor to get him to the nearest A & E.

"I'm okay," he says calmly. "It's just a cut."

I open the passenger door and gently set him down on the seat. Angus brings his foot into his lap to take a look at the damage.

"It's just a cut," he repeats, as I stare at his foot feeling light-headed. "Josh.... Josh, sit down."

With one shaky hand on the car, I lower myself onto the gravel. Everything feels so far away, even Angus's voice sounds like it's coming from a distance.

"Put your head between your knees," he says.

I'm feeling too awful to argue, so I do as he bids.

I breathe deeply and slowly come back to myself.

"Lots of people feel faint at the sight of blood," Angus says kindly as he flips open the tiny medical bag he must have found in the glove compartment.

"I just don't like the thought of how much it hurts," I reply, lifting my head but making sure I keep my gaze on his face. "It's not just the sight of blood… but that it is leaking out of you."

It's not even that I'm thinking about it consciously. I just feel light-headed when I see someone bleeding or in pain, and it's far worse when it's someone I care about. When I hurt Oskar's foot, I didn't feel anything like as bad as I do now, though perhaps I would have if he had been bleeding.

"It reminds me how fragile we are," I add, though I'm not sure where that sentiment comes from all of a sudden. It's not like me to initiate existential conversations.

"I'm not so fragile," Angus says wryly, looking down at his admittedly not particularly fragile-looking frame.

But that's not the sort of fragile I mean. "We're all fragile. Life is, everything. One moment here, the next gone."

"Okay, I agree with that to a certain extent," he says, pulling a thoughtful face. "But perhaps it's the fragility, the temporariness that makes some things precious. Like moments that will never happen again. You have to make them worth it, because even though they are temporary, they are worth happening. If not, what's the point?"

He means it rhetorically, of course, but I don't. "What *is* the point?" I'm not being entirely serious, but in the past I have had this thought, and it has crushed me. Beyond that, sky is just space. We are nothing but momentary sparks in a darkness so endless it belies any *point*.

"Love. Happiness," he states simply, unperturbed, his gaze holding mine. Far surer than his eighteen years suggest he should be.

With the travel tweezers in his hand, Angus focuses again on his foot. I'm still watching his face, thinking about his answer, but I have to glance away when he grimaces with pain.

"Think I might have a bit of glass in it still. It'll be okay if I can get it out."

"Let me take you to hospital."

"And sit around in A & E for the next few hours? No way. I don't want to waste today." His cheeks flush, and he looks quickly away as if he didn't mean to say that, the implications from what he said a moment ago still echoing—*our time together is precious.*

The blush suits him, and I can't help but stare.

"You could get an infection in it," I say.

"That's what this is for." He shows me the tiny tube of antiseptic ointment. "You've never actually opened this kit before, have you?"

"No, thank God. I've not needed to."

"You're much more sensitive about things than you let on, you know."

"And I'd always thought I was hard as nails," I say with a put-upon sigh.

Angus laughs. I want him to do it again.

But at that moment he gasps, and tears run down his cheek. He holds up a tiny bloody shard with the tweezers.

I look away.

"*Ow*," he moans.

Still looking pained, he squeezes out the ointment onto his foot and then opens the pack of bandages with his teeth.

"I'm sorry I'm not being much help," I say, feeling uncomfortable and still a bit woozy.

Angus shrugs. "Neither am I. Stepping on glass isn't exactly the most helpful thing I could have done today."

I watch as he bandages his foot, expecting the blood to soak through, but it doesn't.

When he's finished I reach out and take his ankle in my hand. His expression tells me he has no idea what I am doing, but he doesn't pull back.

I stroke across the ball of his foot, dusting the sand away and massaging gently.

I just want to make him feel good after being in pain. And, strangely, touching him reassures me he's okay.

"Does this hurt?" He shakes his head, not quite looking at me. "Is this okay?"

This time he nods, and I wonder if he's lost his voice.

I've never really considered myself a person who would be in any way turned on by someone's feet, but Angus's are perfectly proportioned—though they're quite wide, they're not too big, his toes and nails are neat and clean, and his skin is soft. I wonder what his skin would feel like against my lips, if he'd find my tongue too ticklish to bear (because I know he's ticklish). I think back to those drunken moments we had in my flat, but the memory is elusive and I can't really remember any of it clearly—only that I wanted him. I've been so stupid.

I smile as Angus shifts as though he's not quite comfortable.

But I don't think he wants me to stop.

I think it's more because today Angus seems to be wearing the tightest trousers known to man. I will myself to stop staring at how closely they hug his legs, the sweet curve of his thighs. With one hand in his lap, he adjusts himself. Again.

"You like your feet being rubbed?" I ask casually. I can't really miss the fact that he's turned on—my face is about a foot from his erection, even if his hand is trying to hide it.

Embarrassment wars with arousal in his eyes, and I'm not sure which feeling wins in the end until he opens his legs a fraction wider, giving me a spectacular view, so I can only assume it's arousal.

"I like being touched." Angus closes his eyes and tilts his head back. "God, that sounds so wrong…."

He swallows, and all I want to do is kiss his throat.

"It doesn't sound wrong." I slip my hand up his tight trouser leg a little to massage his calf, well aware that I may have just crossed a line. I'm carrying on touching him while knowing it turns him on, that he *is* turned on. His legs feel quite hairy, so I'm careful not to press too hard to pull any hair. I just want to give enough pressure to make it pleasurable.

"God, I'm going to be in your lap in a minute." He doesn't look at me as he says this; his head is still tilted away, his eyes still closed, and I can't help the grin that spreads across my face. His talk about making moments worthwhile makes me want to create something worth remembering.

"You're enjoying this, aren't you?" he groans, flopping his head forward and looking at me through slitted eyes.

"Perhaps. Not as much as you, though," I add with a wry smile, ducking as he picks an empty plastic cup off the floor and flings it at me.

Angus shifts again, this time with a wince.

"Want me to stop?" I ask, stilling my hand but keeping hold of his calf.

"No," he says heavily. "Wish I'd put some more comfortable trousers on, though."

"Then I wouldn't be enjoying the view so much."

He swallows again, distinctly uncomfortable this time, and pushes himself upright.

"What?" I ask gently, sensing he's pulling back from me and unable to stop the disappointment I feel.

Angus bites his lip, looking as though he's warring with himself and deciding on whether to tell me something or not.

"Oskar told me I should maybe back off."

"I wonder why," I say heavily, reluctantly withdrawing my hand from his leg.

Oh, I'm aware I told Oskar I wasn't interested in Angus, so I can't really be upset about Oskar's advice.

Angus shakes his head. "He said you were naturally dominant and me coming on to you the whole time might be putting you off. He said you'd probably prefer to be the one doing the chasing—"

Oh. I see.

Dominant? Really? I don't think I have enough experience to exactly know, but I've never thought of myself as particularly dominant. Sure, I like to take the lead in sex, but it's just a preference.

I look up as Angus carries on talking.

"—And I know you probably don't want me to say anything, and it probably defeats the whole object of everything if I tell you, but

I feel better when I'm not hiding anything or trying to. I won't mention it again if you don't want me to but…." The plea in his voice goes straight to my heart. I've knocked him back so many times. I'm such a dick. "I think you already know how much I like you."

The sweet, lopsided smile he gives me has my heart beating heavily and heat pooling in my groin.

"And I really, really like you," he repeats, making me think my reaction to his words must be visible and finding I no longer care.

It's his honesty, his openness with his feelings, that breaks through all my defenses, I realize. It's like an ocean flooding the empty cavities of my heart, filling them, me, with rushing, welcome warmth.

It's as terrifying as drowning and ten times as exhilarating as anything else I've ever felt, and I am becoming too weak to keep on forcing myself to deny these feelings I have for him. I want to surrender to them, lay them down at his feet. I want him to know the fear inside me. I want to finally throw something back at it. Something good. Something like this. Though I still have so much doubt.

"I like you too," I say softly, unable to bring myself to look right at him. "Don't be too hard to get," I add quietly.

I'm hoping he doesn't hear the plea in me, the admission that part of me that's not tied up in knots has wanted to chase him all this time. And at the same time, I know he should hear that. I owe it to him.

Gently, I pick his hand up and move it away from his lap, amazed that he managed to squeeze himself into these trousers at all the way his dick is straining the buttons.

It's a little unfair on him that he can't see how turned on I am right now. But even though it is hidden by my much longer T-shirt, my cock is desperate for some attention. For some of his attention.

I glance around to make sure no one is watching and press the heel of my hand all the way along his erection in one slow stroke. His breath huffs out in little pants, and he bites his lip in an effort to stifle a groan.

"Don't tease me," he pleads, but I can see that even if I told him I *was* teasing him, he wouldn't want me to stop.

"I'm not." I take his hand, locking my fingers briefly with his. "I promise."

After everything, I'm not sure he entirely trusts me, which is not really surprising. Trust is like that—it takes time, its worth needs testing.

"I like that you're so turned on. I just want to make you feel good. But we can stop. I don't want to make you feel vulnerable by doing anything out here."

I let go of his hand and rub my thumb over the head of his cock through his jeans, the heel of my hand pressing against him. I watch his face carefully for any sign he wants me to stop.

He makes a little needy *mmm-mmm-mmm* sound and I close my eyes to slow my breathing down. I want him right here. I wish no one else were around. I wish we were back at home in my flat. I wish I hadn't pushed him away all this time.

"Stop," he says suddenly, gripping his hand over mine, his eyes wide. "I'm going to come." He flushes deeply as he says it.

I lift my hand away and take a deep breath to steady myself.

"Do you really like me?" he asks, his eyes as wide and dark gray as the ocean, his mouth soft and wet from the path of his tongue as he licks his lower lip.

"You have no idea how much I want you right now," I groan, so full of desire it's almost painful not to have him in my arms.

I gesture toward the backseat with my head, and when he nods, I grab his hand and pull him up. I open the back door and help him hop inside to sit on the backseat. Shaking sand off the picnic blanket, I climb in the back of the car with him and drag the blanket across his lap and mine.

We don't kiss, but I want to, God I want to, and I know Angus does too by the way he keeps looking at my lips. I would wait until we get home so we can do this properly, slowly, but I don't think I'm going to be able to see straight enough to drive. My dick is in control of my brain. I pull Angus's hand down to my lap so he can feel it. His fingers scrabble across my stomach and hip, searching, until he finds it—I stifle a moan. Then his fingers slow, stroking delicately, feather light.

With one hard tug, the buttons to his trousers are undone and warm, wet heat is against my fingertips. The front of his thin underwear is so damp, I want to press my face against it, but we're having to do this blind and hidden. I take a peek as I slip my hand inside his underwear, reaching for his balls and finding them nestled painfully in the crease of his trousers.

"Off," I murmur, and Angus obediently shuffles his trousers down until his bare arse is on the car seat, though his nakedness is still hidden by the picnic blanket. It really turns me on sitting next to him like this.

"Better?"

All I get in response is a hot groan against the crook of my neck. The hair at the top of his thighs is so soft and silky against the back of my hand. Angus opens his legs wide as I ignore his dick entirely to cup and stroke his balls. They're large and heavy, and I can tell he likes me touching him like this by the way he's panting. His heart is beating madly—I can feel it hammering against my arm. Emboldened by his reaction, I reach farther back to press against his hole. I just intend to brush against the ring of muscle, but he pushes needily against the pressure, so I spit on my fingertip and rub it around the sensitive area, feeling how tight and tense he is but not quite pushing inside him, just playing with his resistance.

His hand that's not wrapped around his own cock is still lightly tracing the outline of mine, but I know he's too far gone to concentrate on anything but the building sensation.

His eyes are squeezed shut tight, and his expression is one of pained pleasure, so I'm guessing he's close. I watch all his reactions carefully, scared I'm going too fast with him. The quick mutual masturbation in the back of the car I envisaged has turned into something a bit more intense.

If anyone looked in the window right now, they could hardly mistake what we're doing. Angus looks so breathlessly sexy, his full lips slightly parted, so completely uninhibited as I touch him.

I lock my other hand with his as he strokes himself. His thick cock feels amazing, his skin like silk. I rub my thumb across the head, feeling the slickness, spreading it out. It's so different from my dick, and it's been a long time since I've touched anyone else's. I feel the moment he starts to come—the way he goes unbelievably hard and his buttock muscles tighten, the way his mouth opens and he gasps as though he can't breathe. He spurts over my hand, and it soaks into the blanket as he pulses and pulses. I keep stroking until I feel his teeth graze my neck, and I take that as a hint that the sensation is too much.

It's the most intimate sex I've had in years. Without wiping my hand, I reach inside my jeans, smearing Angus's come over my cock. Fuck, it's not going to take long. With a lethargic grin, Angus bats my hand away.

"I want to suck you," he says, still breathless.

"Just your hand," I say shaking my head and burying my face in his hair. Some things I want to save for in private, so I can lose myself. Out here we are far too exposed.

Carefully he unzips my jeans and strokes my cock like he can't get enough of the feel of it, both hands rubbing, quick then slow, hard then soft. I'm so turned on I feel vulnerable, ready to do anything to keep his hands on me. Though I can't quite let go like Angus did—I'm still shocked by how quickly he lost all his inhibitions and trusted me to take care of him like that. None of my quick hookups ever lost it like that.

And I never felt like this.

I grip him tight as I feel my orgasm build and Angus settles into a rhythm, stroking me hard and fast.

As he pulls me over the edge, I feel I am charging through the dark into oblivion. My breath sobs in and out, and I hope that Angus doesn't hear it, that he doesn't know the way I just about broke inside.

We keep our arms around each other. I'm afraid to pull away, afraid to face his expression. Afraid to face the world outside of this moment, the line I have crossed.

"People say first times are always crap. They are so wrong," he whispers, and I can hear the way he is smiling, feel it against my skin.

"That was your first time?" I swallow, pulling back to look at him.

He looks completely elated and so sexy and warmly inviting—all dark eyes and swollen lips—whereas I'm feeling pretty crap that his first time was a quickie in the back of my falling-apart car.

"Yeah." Again he looks as though he wants to say something more but he doesn't.

His face and neck are still flushed with arousal and I know he could probably go another round (as perhaps could I), but not here.

"We should, um, clean up," I say gently, sensing movement, people nearby.

What we just did was a little reckless, and being reckless isn't really my thing. I wipe myself with a tissue and zip my jeans back up, still feeling sticky and a little gross.

"You're not… you don't… regret it?" Angus asks hesitantly as I open the door to get out.

"Not a single fucking second," I say thickly, my gaze fixed on his.

Chapter 9

"I THINK you should get your foot checked out to make sure it's not infected," I say as we're driving back toward London. "You never know what sort of crap is chucked in the sea. There could be sewage, anything."

"And I was thinking you taking me to see the sea was all romantic."

Angus can't stop smiling. I don't think he's stopped since… well, since we got each other off in the back of the car.

It's only early afternoon, but already the sunlight is hazy as we drive across the downs. I can't remember a more beautiful winter's day—clear and cold, the world icily defined at the edges, the colors all muted greens and grays.

I try to keep my eyes on the road, but I know Angus keeps looking at me. I don't mind, I just… don't know. Every time I catch his eye, I feel a giddy rush of *something*, as though I'm back at school crushing on someone so hard it takes my breath away. And it is ridiculous to feel like that at twenty-five, so fucking ridiculous, but at the same time, it's wonderful, and there is no way I want it to stop.

We don't talk much. The tension between us is nice, and I don't want to spoil it with my stupid mouth. I can't believe how utterly beautiful he is. How he can possibly want the same thing I do. But my dick is still mostly in charge of my brain and I am running with how good this feels for once. Maybe I'm still feeling the effects of being ill. Maybe it has canceled out my sense of self-preservation—or perhaps just my sense.

"Have you got time for a detour before we go home?" Angus asks as we reach the outskirts of London. "I want to show you something."

His tone is light, though I can sense an undercurrent here, a deeper motivation, but he's still smiling, so I nod.

I am never this easy. I've never been this easy in my entire life. But right now it's as if I'm in the middle of the stream instead of clinging to the bank. It's drawing me along, and it feels good. Because of Angus, it feels so good.

"Head toward Selhurst and then Thornton Heath," he says pointing at the signs as we drive through Croydon.

Once we reach Thornton Heath high street, the traffic becomes a lot heavier, and Angus tells me where to turn off and guides me through back streets without even seeming to think about it.

He knows this area. He knows it really well.

For the first time in an hour, Angus's smile begins to slip.

We turn into an estate. There are three square tower blocks around a central car park and a few short streets of two-story maisonettes dwarfed beneath them. It's not the most run-down estate I've seen, but it's not the nicest either. It still makes me feel paranoid and as if I should check I've locked the car doors.

There is a kids' play park, but it looks mostly dismantled, and we get stared at as we pass by the dozen or so kids standing around the outside of it.

I pull over down one of the side streets and turn the engine off.

"This is where your dad lives, isn't it? This is where you grew up."

"I just wanted to show you," Angus says quietly. "But now I'm here, I wish I hadn't come."

"Why?" I ask softly.

"Bad memories."

He draws his bare feet up and rests them on the dashboard. If we were back in the alternate universe we usually inhabit, I would tell him to take them down. Instead I take hold of his hand as he stares straight ahead out the windscreen.

"I'd like to see it," I say. "I'd like to see where you lived."

"I don't want to get out of the car," he says. "Just drive past."

"Okay."

The house is on the next street over. It's not the worst house on the street. It just looks a little uncared for and neglected. A leaking drainpipe has watermarked the brickwork above the front door. The tiny front garden is haphazardly paved, with the occasional weed poking through. A pair of faded curtains are drawn across the downstairs window so that we can't see inside. The upstairs window just looks blank and dark.

I try to imagine Angus living here, but I don't like to think of him unhappy. Angus sinks lower in his seat and folds his arms across his chest as we pass by.

"I never told you why I left, not really," he whispers. "Mum doesn't even know why."

I'm surprised because Angus doesn't seem to be the type to hold on to secrets. He's the sort of person who needs to get everything out there in the open to deal with it. This could be why he's telling me, though, because he does need to get it out, because keeping it in is hurting him. So I keep driving, just around and around the estate, knowing he'll probably find it easier to talk if my whole focus isn't solely on him.

"Mum thinks I was so angry at him about the college thing that I finally got the balls to tell him I hated living with him and was going to live with her instead." Angus shakes his head, his expression displaying a bitter self-hatred I know far too intimately. "But it wasn't like that. I didn't confront him about anything. I'm too much of a coward for that. Instead I ran away. Just took off one night. That's why I was so afraid when he started hanging around. I'm so fucking weak. He'd just have to tell me to get in the car and go with him, and I probably would."

I steal another quick glance, not wanting to take my eyes off this obstacle course of a street for more than half a second. Angus may think he's weak, but that's not my impression at all, especially not these past few weeks with all the crap he's dealt with. For a while he just stares out the window.

"Did something happen to make you run?" I prompt gently, sensing there is more to this story.

"Have you ever had someone be disappointed in you, and yet you know what disappoints them is just who you are and you can't do anything about it?"

I stop the car and meet Angus's gaze, but I can't answer that or think too deeply about it without opening up a whole lot of pain about my own past.

"I've spent my life trying not to disappoint my dad. But he was disappointed with everything about me—with how I turned out, with how much I'm like my mum sometimes. That I'm shy, that I… I get emotional, though I tried so hard to hide it because he thinks it's pathetic. And then one day I realized I was never not going to disappoint him. It just wasn't going to happen. What disappoints him is who I am," he says miserably.

"You are not weak," I say solemnly.

Right now he's once again proving how strong and determined he is. He's pushing the boundaries between us, bringing us closer together, the way only revealing secrets can. I take his hand, and I squeeze it tightly.

Angus stares at our joined hands.

"I wanted to go somewhere I could be myself for once. Somewhere I wasn't constantly on guard and having to hide. I wanted to explore what it meant to be *gay*"—he whispers the word—"and if that's what I really was."

I get the impression *this* is the crux of it.

"So are you?" I say, giving him a half smile despite myself, unable to stop the flood of thoughts that assault me—Angus in my arms earlier, inhibitions blown out to sea.

Angus huffs out a laugh and rolls his eyes. "What do you think?"

I hold his gaze. His eyes are beautiful, I know I've thought this before, but they really are—the delicate tilted shape of them, the unusual color. I remember when I first saw him, it was his mass of near-black hair that caught my attention, and I kind of missed the way he shone beneath it.

"You hide behind your hair," I say gently, letting my finger trace his jaw. "And you really shouldn't."

"I'm not confident like you."

I frown. *Since when did I become the epitome of confidence?*

"I guess we all have things we hide behind," I say.

The admission has barbs, and I try not to wince as they dig deep.

I know he sees so much more of who I am than everyone else, but I long to tell him that with me, it's *all* a front. So much front I'm scared there's nothing real behind it anymore.

And I realize I have no right to tell him not to hide.

"I don't want to hide anymore. One day I want to have the courage to look him in the eye and just be myself."

When Angus says this, it makes me want to turn the car around and go and confront that bastard of a father who has made his pure, beautiful son feel so ashamed of who he is. It's so fucking wrong.

"Are you angry?"

Taking a deep breath, I let go of Angus's hand and start the car. If I don't move, I might end up doing something stupid.

"There's a thing or two I'd like to say to your dad," I reply tightly.

"Don't," Angus says quietly. "Just… can you please take me home now, Josh?"

I know he doesn't want to be anywhere near this place anymore. With a heavy heart, I put my foot down and drive away, heading mostly on instinct toward home.

THE WHOLE journey back, my gut is in knots. Angus doesn't speak at all, and whenever I glance over at him, he looks lost in thought, his head resting against the window, his eyes staring at nothing.

It's just about dark when we arrive home. I kill the engine as soon as we pull up outside the house, and we sit in silence, making no move to get out of the car.

All in all it's been a strange day. Though there are definitely some parts of it that will be replaying in my head tonight.

My anger at Angus's father has somehow squashed any ideas I had of dragging Angus up to my flat—my bed—for a rerun of earlier. But perhaps that is for the best. I don't want to rush things with him—if there is even anything to rush—and if that was his first time, he probably needs some space to get his head around it before he decides he actually *wants* a rerun.

I need to get my head around it too. In a big way.

But I have no desire to run right now, no desire to push him away.

"Come on, I'll help you inside," I say eventually. "With your injury, you and Oskar will have a matching set," I add, trying to lighten the mood.

Angus looks at me gratefully—perhaps for just letting go of what we were talking about and not going on about my feelings for his father.

"You sure you haven't got some weird foot thing?" he asks wryly, leaning into me as he hops. We make our way cautiously across the cold pavement, looking out for any other sharp objects. I take as much of his weight as he will let me and carry his shoes in my free hand.

"A fetish?"

Angus blushes. It strikes me as funny that he can be so uninhibited during sex and yet so shy talking about it.

"It's just a word."

"I know," he says coyly.

"Looking at my flat, I've probably got some sort of word fetish or book fetish, though." I'm not actually being serious, but for a moment I do wonder if it's true.

"Maybe I've got one for you," Angus says quietly.

Though his head is down, I can see him smiling through his sheaf of hair.

"That's not a fetish—that's just the normal reaction to my presence," I whisper jokingly, thinking for a second that I sound just like Soren.

As I grip my arm around him tighter and feel his muscles tense beneath my fingertips, suddenly I become aware of how good he feels pressed against me, how good he smells, all sea washed and windblown, how his dark hair…. Fuck, at this rate we are definitely going to end up in my bed tonight.

"Want a hand?" a voice calls, interrupting my thoughts.

Oskar stands at the front door, looking concerned. He must have been watching us through the window. How he thinks he's going to be any help with his broken foot, I have no idea. I suspect he just wants to get in the way. Although he did give Angus some well-intended, if not kind of strange advice about where he was going wrong with me, so maybe he's not trying to. Maybe he's just worried about Angus.

"I stood on some glass when we were on the beach," Angus tells Oskar as he comes to offer his shoulder for Angus to lean on.

We continue up the path, Angus sandwiched between us. I roll my eyes. I was managing quite well supporting Angus on my own.

"Want me to take a look?" Oskar asks once we're inside Eleanor's flat.

I'm surprised to see the place looks a lot tidier than it did a week ago. Angus's notes are no longer strewn like paper tiles across the floor. The washing up is done and put away. The place even smells fresher, as though someone has opened a window once or twice.

I lead Angus over to the sofa. I feel a little useless—I can't help check his injury.

"I should go… get some stuff ready to eat," I say, watching uncomfortably as Oskar sits down and begins to peel Angus's bandage off his foot.

"Okay," Angus says slowly, not taking his eyes off me. I get the impression he's trying to tell me he understands. "You could come back down later maybe, or I could…?"

He leaves the words hanging as if he wants me to finish off the sentence, but I can't, not with Oskar here. I don't know why.

"Yeah, maybe," I say.

I blink at him, hoping he'll understand I'm not brushing him off, it's just the complicated mess that is my brain refusing to cooperate. I'm not sure he gets it, but as Oskar hisses in a breath of sympathy at the sight of Angus's cut, I turn around and leave them to it.

As I walk upstairs, I wonder why I can't quite let myself jump into this with both feet like the giddy rejoicing part of me wants to. When it's just me and Angus, I feel more and more sure of him—amazed by how well we fit together on some deep level, thrilled to be close to him, every one of my nerve endings set on fire by his presence. But when anyone else is around or I'm on my own, that certainty starts to recede and I'm back where I started, wondering what I've got to offer anyone apart from heartache—and Angus deserves so much more than that—and wondering why anyone in their right mind would want to be in a relationship anyway, giving anyone else that sort of dangerous power over their heart.

Of course, then comes the confusing knowledge that it doesn't matter what you want or however much you try to fight it—if you fall in love, they have that power anyway.

Chapter 10

I WAKE up almost twelve hours later with a dry mouth and a head feeling as though it's made of concrete that had been left out in the baking sun. I lie blinking at the light shining in through the living room windows, trying to piece last night back together and finding I have nothing. I'm in the clothes I wore yesterday, and I've slept on the sofa all night. I don't even think I dreamed.

Slowly, the whole of yesterday starts to come back to me, particularly the parts with Angus in the back of the car, particularly the warm weight of him in my arms, the scent of his skin. My cock stiffens at the memory. It's a memory I could think on for a good long while—he turns me on so completely—but I don't let myself. It would feel disrespectful somehow, getting off on that memory, using it, when really what I need to do is sort out my feelings about the whole situation.

I don't regret it. Surprising myself, I acknowledge I don't regret any of it, but now that I've slept on it, it's hard to see it happening again. It's hard to see me letting down my defenses enough for it to happen again. I'm not sure what happened yesterday to break through them.

Perhaps if I hadn't curled up on my sofa, the velvet soft against my cheek, and fallen asleep, I really would have gone back downstairs. Perhaps I would have just gone for it and invited Angus back to my flat, where we would have had one of those sweet and achy first-time fucks that I've written about all over my kitchen walls. Perhaps a lot of things would have happened.

But it didn't, and all I know now is that I care for Angus deeply and his friendship alone is no longer enough. The thought of him with anyone else makes my guts twist painfully and my heart tighten as though I'm having a panic attack (and it's been years since I've had one of those).

If this goes wrong, it will fuck me up completely. There is no way it will not. But this self-sabotage has to stop. Perhaps I need to talk to him, be open, though I don't know if I can.

Rolling off the sofa, I wait for my head to stop spinning before I check the time again, and get ready for work.

After a few minutes of indecision, I knock on Angus's door before I leave. I just want to explain that I fell asleep last night, and I didn't change my mind or regret anything. I wait for a minute or two, but nobody answers, so I leave, thinking Angus and Oskar are probably still asleep. There is a doubtful little voice that tells me they could be sleeping together—Angus could have been upset because he thought I knocked him back last night and needed some comfort—but that voice withers under my steady internal glare.

Angus is better than that—I know he is. Relationships that crumble because of jealousy or pathetic misunderstandings are never going to last.

I'M TIRED. The strain of yesterday, and still being weak from illness, makes finding the strength to do anything hard. But I make it through the day. Even though Soren is not a particularly sympathetic person, I know he's watching me. I know he gives me the easy jobs to do, and he even refrains from leaving me to cope alone when it's his lunch hour and he's perfectly entitled to spend it away from the shop.

Despite his annoying habit of acting as though he has a right to know everything about everyone's personal life, Soren doesn't ask how my day at the beach went or if I even went to the beach.

What's even more surprising is that if he asks, I'll probably tell him. I've not stopped thinking about it.

There is still some weird excitement bubbling up inside me whenever I think about Angus. I don't know what's going to happen with him. I don't even know what it is I *want* to happen with him, but for the first time in my life it's the not known that I'm excited about—it's the possibilities.

I DRIVE home quickly after work. Anticipation is making my heart beat wildly against my rib cage as if in an effort to escape my chest.

Betrayed by my body again, I think with a half-giddy, half-heavy sigh.

Angus is on the front steps of the house, all wrapped up and waiting for me. He phoned me earlier and we arranged to go and see Eleanor together this evening. I thought going straight after work again would be the best idea and that way it would leave the evening free for… for whatever.

"How is your foot?" I ask, trying my utmost to act all calm and collected as he slips into the passenger seat beside me. I noticed he was hobbling a little as he walked down the path.

"Sore, but I can walk on it okay."

I nod, banishing a vivid image of his foot all covered in blood yesterday.

I'm a mess of impulses. I'm finding it hard to make my brain work now he's near me after thinking about him nonstop all day. I switch on the windscreen wipers by accident as I try to find something to do with my hand. The wipers protest noisily, and I feel my skin heating.

I never blush. *Never, never, never*. Crap.

Worst of all, I can't tell if the buzz I'm feeling is just one-sided or if it's coming from him as well.

The air feels charged between us, and if it's not one-sided, Angus must be trying to ignore the hell out of it too.

"You all studied out for the test tomorrow?" I ask, changing the subject.

"Yeah, no more or I think my brain will explode into one-sentence fragments." He laughs, his cold breath visible in the freezing evening air.

I stare at his mouth and think about kissing him.

"I hope you weren't waiting outside for long. I rushed back from work, but traffic is a bitch at this time of day." Impulsively I reach out and squeeze his hand—his fingers are like sticks of ice. It seems my body is going for it even if my brain is ten steps behind. "You'll be fine tomorrow, you know. I've never known anyone be as prepared as you are."

"We'll see," he says, giving me half a smile and squeezing my fingers back.

AFTER WE sign in at the hospital, one of the psychiatric doctors comes out to have a quiet word with us. Angus frowns worriedly as she leads us into a small insipid-colored side room and closes the door. The room is decked out like a miniature consulting room, with a small desk and two chairs. She gestures at the two chairs. We don't sit down. I sense Angus is more on edge than I am, wondering what the hell is wrong.

"I'm Yvonne Marshall," the doctor tells us, holding out her hand. "I'm a director of mental health at St. George's Hospital, but I also work with patients here twice a week."

The introduction is unnecessary. Her name badge displays who she is. I just want her to get on with it, tell us what has happened. We're not in some game show where they have to flick to the adverts to keep the audience on edge. We are already on edge.

Then I realize, from the purposeful direction of her gaze, the introduction was for me. She seems to know Angus.

"Josh. I'm a friend of the family," I tell her.

"He's staying," Angus says adamantly, as if he can guess what Yvonne might suggest.

Yvonne nods, possibly as surprised as I am at the determination evident in his tone.

"As I think I made you aware the last time we spoke, Angus, we don't use sedatives as a method for managing anxiety here. But if a patient does become particularly anxious, we will sedate them to enable them to talk about their feelings and what caused the problem so that they can be better equipped to deal with it next time. It's all about management."

Her words make me tense, causing a strange sensation of déjà vu.

It's all about management, having strategies in place that help you deal with life, mechanisms that help you cope...

don't feel

don't feel

don't feel

"Why did you sedate her?" Angus asks, bringing me back to the moment at hand.

"Her anxiety escalated this afternoon. She explained afterwards she was expecting you to visit her during afternoon visiting hours, and when you didn't she was concerned something had happened to you. I think it all stems back to how worried she is about you because of the burglary."

"But I told Mum I was going to visit this evening with Josh. I have an exam tomorrow and I wanted to spend the day studying and the bus takes ages so Josh offered to drive me if we came in together later," Angus explains in a rush, clearly distressed.

Without thinking, I grip his hand, locking our fingers together. He would hate the thought of being the cause of his mum suffering, even though Eleanor's anxiety is not his fault in any way. It's only when I notice the fleeting, curious look Yvonne gives us that I realize what I am doing and let go of his hand.

"I think she must have forgotten," Yvonne says kindly. "Please don't blame yourself. Your mum is suffering from a serious anxiety disorder that has completely affected the way she functions. Her reactions to normal events are extreme, and as I explained the other day, I'm hopeful we can normalize those reactions. But I thought you should know before your visit that she won't be as responsive to you today."

Yvonne leaves us to make our own way across the common room to Eleanor's room. Angus looks miserable.

I tug him to one side before we get there.

"It's not your fault," I say, my hand on his shoulder, squeezing lightly, feeling the gentle movement of his muscles beneath all the layers of fabric he's wearing and wishing I could touch his skin.

"I know. In my head I know. But knowing in your head doesn't make your heart feel any better, does it?"

I shake my head in agreement, feeling his words sink much deeper than perhaps he meant them to.

TODAY, INSTEAD of sitting in one of the chairs, Eleanor is tucked beneath the covers in bed. And whereas the chairs and other pieces of furniture resemble items that could feasibly be found in a living room, the adjustable bed advertises itself as pure hospital equipment.

The thin bedclothes emphasize Eleanor's small frame, and she seems so tiny and fragile. But her face is relaxed and her expression peaceful, making her look younger and more like the woman she was when I met her, years ago.

"We can just sit with her for a bit," I say as Angus stops woodenly at the foot of the bed. "Sometimes sedatives can make you appear asleep when you're not. Just talk to her, tell her about your exam tomorrow. She'll be so proud. She'll know you've been to visit—don't worry."

Angus pulls a chair up to her bedside. I hesitate for a moment, then pull a chair up next to him.

"Do you want a minute on your own?" I ask when he doesn't move or say anything.

"No, I'm just thinking."

"What about?" I ask gently, berating myself for being as nosy as Soren.

"You," he says simply.

My heartbeat quickens, a bird's wing-flutter. *If I placed his hand over my heart, would he feel it?* I wonder.

"Thank you for being here," he carries on.

"I want to be here."

Angus takes Eleanor's hand where it lies against the bedclothes. Then he takes mine. For a while we sit like that silently. When Angus starts to speak, telling Eleanor about the studying he's been doing and his exam tomorrow, I squeeze his hand tighter and rub small circles against the soft skin of his inner wrist with my thumb.

We stay for perhaps half an hour. We're about to leave when I see Eleanor's eyelids flutter open.

Angus gets up and hugs her without saying a word.

"I love you," she says to him, and I know that's what he needs to hear.

"I love you too, Mum. Try not to worry about me. I'm going to leave you a note about when I'm coming to see you tomorrow, okay?"

His voice is hoarse, and I know he's trying not to cry.

Eleanor nods, but at the mention of us leaving, even though it is with a promise of return, her expression grows serious and morose.

"Josh?"

She beckons me closer, and Angus stands up and backs away, wiping his eyes with his sleeve. Her arms come around me, and she hugs me too.

"Don't work too hard," she murmurs, making me feel guilty that I haven't been to see her for a few days. I think Angus was right to lie and tell her I was working overtime—if she knew I was sick, she would worry about him all the more. She would worry I wasn't watching over him. Sometimes, perhaps such deception is necessary.

She touches my cheek and frowns. "You look tired."

So often she has cared for me in the ways my own mother failed. All I want is for her to be okay, to be able to live the life she wants without every day being a battle for her to get through. Because I know that's what it's like when life falters and nothing is simple.

I stroke her hair back. "I'm okay. I'm looking out for him," I mouth, not wanting Angus to hear what I'm saying.

"I'm happy for you two," she whispers a little drowsily.

I turn and give Angus a brief quizzical look before leaning closer to hear her continue.

“You’ve taken good care of me, Josh. I know you will take good care of my son.” Even though she is whispering, I am sure Angus can hear every word.

Though neither of us has said or done anything in particular to make Eleanor think there is something going on between us, it feels strangely like being given her blessing.

Chapter 11

ANGUS IS much happier on the way home. Not quite carefree, but every so often he glances at me and grins.

"What?" I ask as we speed through the blackness of South London.

Angus shakes his head, smiling to himself.

"You're distracting me," I tell him, thinking how beautiful he looks, how lit up inside he becomes every time he smiles.

"It's going to be okay," he says cryptically.

"Well, I'm glad we got that sorted out, then." I pull a wry face at him and turn into our street.

"I mean it," Angus says once I've pulled over and turned the engine off. "I've got this feeling everything's going to be okay."

Without giving me a chance to contemplate what on earth he's going on about, Angus pushes his hair out of his eyes, leans across the gear stick, and kisses me. *I guess he decided to ignore Oskar's advice, after all* is the only thought that enters my mind before I am drowning in the velvet crush of his lips, the slick heat of his mouth and tongue. He lifts one of his hands to cup my ear, stroking the skin around it with such gentle tenderness and reverence, I am undone. He touches me and kisses openmouthed as though this is his one and only chance to pull me away from oblivion, from the emptiness that has so often threatened to surround me, inside and out. He kisses me as though this is what he was always meant to do. And I am burning up for him, star bright. I cover his hand with my own and let the sensation of his tongue lapping against mine cancel out any other thought.

I am lost. I long to pull him into my lap so I can lock our bodies together. I want him so much that I have no doubt we could get each other off like this. But we're in my car, parked outside our house on a residential South London street, and I have to pull away. Though I don't pull back far, I knock my forehead against his, our hands still gripping tightly.

"I think—" I take a deep breath, suddenly realizing I need air as much as the next human. "—we need to go somewhere more private, so we can do things that require a lot less clothing."

Angus groans. His breath as erratic as mine. Breathing is such a forgettable task in the face of blazing desire, and bigger, deeper feelings I cannot name, only surrender to.

He kisses the corner of my mouth, and everything else is forgotten—we can't seem to stop searching for each other's lips, tasting, exploring. His hands are in my hair, stroking the back of my neck. His touch so light, it makes me weak, makes me desperate for more.

"Angus—" The word comes out halfway between a gasp and a moan. "—come on."

We exit the car, slam the doors—I barely remember to lock them—and cling tightly to each other's hands as we hurry up the path. We barely make it to the stairs before Angus's hand cups the back of my head and his mouth finds mine again. We're right outside his flat, so I tug him with me and we stumble the rest of the way upstairs.

I can't find the right key for my door. There is only a choice of three—car key, communal front door key, flat key—but I am so distracted. Angus has pushed open my coat and lifted my jumper, and his hand is now ghosting across my hip, his fingers tracing swirls across my bare skin. I lean against the door, pull him into my arms, and give up. How the hell can he turn me into such a boneless mass of want? He's never even done this before.

We could kiss like this for hours—I want to kiss like this for hours—but I'm not taking it further on the stairs. We need privacy for that. Leaning his forehead against mine, he takes the keys out of my hand and stares at them for a minute, frowning.

"Which key?" he asks, and it pleases me to hear the desperate edge to his voice.

"Your fault I can't think straight," I tell him, grabbing back the keys and taking a deep breath to concentrate on putting the right one in the lock. It's really not so fucking hard to do when my dick isn't blindly driving every single thought and impulse.

We fall through the doorway. I push Angus up hard against the wall, thinking there's no way we're going to make it to bed—not this time. I capture his mouth with mine, kissing him desperately while my fingers work the buttons of his jeans and he struggles out of his coat. The way we're both trying to frantically rid each other of our clothes strikes me as funny, and breaking the kiss, I laugh breathlessly. Angus grins at my amusement. The tension between us changing, slowing, but only a little.

"God we're pathetically desperate for each other, aren't we?" I say, cupping his face and looking deep into the dark of his eyes.

"I want to tell you something. I need you to know," Angus whispers, searching my eyes and straining up to kiss me lightly.

The whole of my body presses tight against his. The tiny rocking movement of our hips causes sensations at once desperately sweet and wonderfully achy.

"Maybe I already know," I whisper back, before licking his lower lip and sucking it into my mouth. Words will only make me think, reevaluate, and I don't want to stop.

Still kissing him, I one-handedly push his jeans and pants down and take the warm, hard length of his cock in my hand. Gently I sweep my thumb across the head, slicking precome across his skin. With a cut-off gasp, Angus sucks my tongue deep into his mouth, and I begin to lose control. I shove my own trousers down, needing to feel my cock against his, hot skin to hot skin.

I pull away, wanting eye contact as I stroke us together. The feel of him against me, the reality of it, is making it hard to breathe. We're still mostly fully clothed—tops, jumpers, our trousers around our knees—but this moment is so pure and so intimate, I feel utterly naked, utterly without anything to hide behind, and I don't think I want to hide any longer.

Not from him.

"Come in my mouth," I groan, dropping to my knees as I feel him beginning to tense like he did in the back of the car.

I take him as deep as I can, cupping his tightening balls with one hand and pumping the base of his cock with the other. He thrusts his hips once, throws his head back, and comes, liquid warmth filling my mouth. I pull off slightly to taste him, sucking and licking until he's fully spent. I want to hold his cock in my mouth until his orgasm fades completely, but his legs begin to tremble, then buckle, and I guide him down onto my lap, listening to his breathing slow.

"Did you come?" he asks after a moment, blinking at me, his face and neck still flushed.

I raise my eyebrows, my arms completely full of this unbelievably sexy, half-naked young man.

"I've wanted to… to suck you off for forever," he carries on, stumbling over the words but saying them all the same.

"We've got all night," I whisper before kissing his neck.

With the greatest of care, I help him out of his T-shirt and jumper and then his shoes and trousers. Angus sits on the floor naked, and for a moment he looks a little awkward and shy, but his cock is already plumping up, ready for round two. I forget how many times you can go at eighteen, when your recovery time is counted in minutes rather than hours. Well, we can work around that.

"I love your cock." I smile, staring at it, watching him harden, his foreskin stretching as the head colors and swells. "Really turns me on seeing you getting turned on again."

I know those words will make him blush—it's entirely why I say them.

I run my finger up from the base, watching how his stomach muscles tighten and his cock straightens rapidly.

"Help me out of my clothes," I say breathlessly.

I can't remember the last time I was completely naked with someone. Hookups are all about getting off. There is no tenderness, no need to strip off completely. It's funny that I thought that would ever be enough—funny, because as Angus slowly pulls my T-shirt off over my head, his expression so vulnerable and intent and so full of desire, I know only this will ever be enough.

Only this. Only him.

I take his hand and lead him to the bedroom.

MY DESIRE is a slow burn, a slow movement of my hips, my cock rubbing a wet trail against the hard muscles of Angus's stomach or battling with his much thicker cock for the tight spot between our hips. We kiss deep and slow, our fingers stroking one another, touching everywhere. I can barely hold back my excitement as Angus strokes down between my buttocks, blindly seeking that sensitive ring of muscle, mirroring what I did to him in the car. He is hesitant, and I haven't always enjoyed being touched like this in the past, but when Angus's finger presses against me, I push my hips back to meet him, to welcome his invasion, wanting something of him inside me, and our kisses become much deeper and more desperate than before. I want him to bring me off like that, one finger deep within me, his mouth making a delicious mess of my cock as I come.

"Please suck my cock," I gasp, breaking the kiss.

Angus grabs my hand as he licks down my stomach and tangles our fingers together in his hair.

"Show me what to do," he whispers, looking up at me with wide darkened eyes, rubbing his smooth cheek against my cock. Gripping my hand tighter in his hair, I guide his mouth, lifting my hips so that I slide between his lips, enveloped in wet heat. I can feel his tongue dancing, exploring. His breath heavy against my skin. I love the way he's letting me do this, letting me guide him and control the movement. I love the wet sounds he makes as he sucks. But most of all, it's watching him—seeing my dick disappear between his swollen lips and watching him jerk off as he does it.

It doesn't take long to bring me to the edge. I don't hold back.

"Angus," I groan, though I'm almost too late with my warning, my hips jerking already. I try and loosen my grip on his hair so he doesn't choke and can pull back if he wants to—not everyone likes to swallow—but he doesn't pull back, instead he opens his mouth and lets me watch as I spill all over his tongue. It's perhaps the hottest thing I've ever seen. Especially when he squeezes his eyes shut a second later and grunts as he comes over his fist.

"I like the way you taste," he says, crawling up the bed.

I push away the thick sheaf of hair that falls in front of his eyes, wanting, needing to see him clearly.

"So what do I taste of?" I want to encourage his boldness, even though his shyness turns me on.

But Angus closes his eyes and instead presses his tongue against mine.

We lose ourselves in each other. At some point we take a shower together, and I bring him off slow and intense, with my tongue laving a thick path from the base of his spine to his balls as he crouches on his hands and knees, offering himself up to me. He asks me to fuck him. But what we're doing is just as intimate. I want him to know there is more to sex than some guy's dick inside you.

When he whispers he loves me, I pretend not to hear. It's too soon. But I know I have never felt closer to anyone, and every little touch my body makes against his holds more truth than any words.

Chapter 12

SUNLIGHT WAKES me.

I am curled beside him, my arms wound around his naked chest, pulling him close. I love the silky feel of his chest hair. Even after last night, his body is a wonder to me. My erection presses in the smooth crease of his backside, but I don't want to do anything about it other than hold him, locked in this moment I somehow know I will remember until the end.

But it doesn't last. How can it?

I'm scared as I lie there, and I don't know how not to be. I'm scared that this is temporary and I will lose him, because ultimately I know that it is, and I will. Surely there can be no name for what I feel. No word enough to describe this exhilaration and disbelief. My heart swelled, wanting to share itself, give itself, to him.

But I don't know how to deal with the fear these feelings bring—the terror and the emptiness that threaten should this all disintegrate and I find myself holding tight to nothing.

Sleepily, he blinks and reaches for me, presses his closed lips against mine, and smiles—a sweet hello. I pull away and stroke his wild brown hair, the ends turning gold in the morning light.

I know Angus feels no fear lying here with me, but I can tell he senses mine.

"Are you okay?" he whispers, his voice a little croaky, concern evident in his gray gaze.

I nod, unable to speak. There is a pressure building inside me, and I don't know how to stop it.

I run my fingers down his cheek, tracing the shape of his lips, his nose. He's so utterly beautiful. How can he be here with me? I don't deserve this. How can it ever work? It's too fragile. Everything is so fragile.

"What time is your exam?" I ask eventually. Perhaps bringing normality into this will make it easier to accept.

"Not until two thirty this afternoon." He pulls a stricken face. "Tell me it's not this afternoon!"

I smile. Or at least try to. "It's just before seven," I say without looking at a clock.

Angus quirks his lips, puzzled. "You're guessing."

"I watch the light, where it is in the room. I always wake up about the same time, though I still set an alarm. It goes off at seven."

As if on cue, the alarm starts bleeping. I reach across Angus to stop it, pausing longer than I need to, my whole body pressed against his.

Still the pressure builds in my chest, my throat. I feel choked. Overwhelmed.

"I've got work at nine," I say, disentangling myself and getting up.

I don't want Angus to notice I'm losing it.

I've never felt so close to being complete and yet so close to completely breaking apart. I don't know how to deal with it. *If* I can deal with it even.

I take my clothes into the bathroom to get dressed. I refuse to break down in front of Angus, but something inside me is definitely breaking.

ANGUS IS dressed by the time I vacate the bathroom, though his T-shirt is inside out and his confidence is wavering.

"Good luck for later," I say before kissing his cheek and giving him a quick hug.

He seems reluctant, but he takes the hint and makes for the front door. Once he's reached it, he stops, and I can see him building up the courage to say something. I'm willing him with everything in me to just go. I need him to just go.

But of course he doesn't.

"You sure you're okay…? Because… because you don't seem yourself and this is kind of momentous for me too and I'd understand if you feel overwhelmed but I'm so scared right now. I'm scared that once you shut this door you're never going to open it to me again," he finishes, sounding breathless.

His hands are shaking.

I should be honest. If only because I'll hurt him if I'm not. And I care about him deeply. I can't deny that. This is hard.

"I'm not pushing you away."

"Okay. But you are," he says, his head down.

This is no good.

And he's right, last night was momentous. I will never forget it.

I tilt his head back up, stroking my thumb against the soft hair of his cheek, dark and unshaven. I move in close to lean my forehead against his. The scent of his skin is sexy, reminding me of everything we did last night, how well explored we are, the taste of him still on my tongue.

I want to tell him I just need to get my head around this, around my feelings for him, because I've never felt like this about anyone before. I want to tell him I'm scared, that there is a part of me that's screaming I can't trust this—my feelings, his feelings, any of it—and it is so hard to ignore. But I can't say those words.

Instead I kiss him, softly, tenderly, wishing again to show him what I mean without words. It is a far more eloquent form of communication.

Angus's response is to tangle his fingers in my hair and squeeze his eyes shut tight, returning my kiss in earnest. If this were just about sex, it would be so damn easy.

"Call me or text me and let me know how your exam goes," I say as he makes his way downstairs.

I hear him make some sound of assent before I close my door and lean against it.

Trust was never going to come easy for me. After everything, it is perhaps the hardest thing of all. I look up at the ceiling, at the vast emptiness of space described there—the reality of our insignificance is mind-blowing.

But a voice that sounds so much like Angus tells me how that only makes it all the more amazing that we are here, that we have found each other as we're spinning through the darkness.

Chapter 13

I'M DEALING with a customer when Oskar hobbles into the shop on crutches. He sits down on one of the solid leather stools in the middle and waits to be served. The jeans and top he's wearing are a little loose on his skinny frame, and it occurs to me they must belong to Angus.

I'm not sure why Oskar is here, but I'm pretty certain he's not come in to buy a pair of overpriced shoes.

Soren is fucking around out the back trying to get one of the electronic foot scanners to work, and I'm glad he's not out here. He'd work out in no time that this is the Oskar whose foot I ran over, and he'd think he had free rein to ask all manner of invasive questions.

My customer leaves, and I try and school my wary expression into a more welcoming one.

"Want me to measure you up?" I ask.

Oskar gives me a strange look and shakes his head. "I just came to talk to you about Angus."

"Can't it wait? I'm at work." I don't mean to be so offhand with him—it just comes out.

"I don't really want him to know I came to see you. I can wait until you've finished."

He seems so uncertain of me. I think he perhaps believes me to be as harsh as I sound.

"Are you here to warn me off?" I ask.

"Why would you think that?" He practically shrinks.

I shrug and sit down on the stool next to him. "I lied to you about not having any feelings for Angus." The words just come out. It's not as hard as I imagined.

"I kind of didn't believe you anyway."

I sigh, nudging him with my shoulder, mostly amiably, because even if Oskar didn't believe me about my feelings, he still kissed Angus and offered to suck him off. And yeah, it hurts, even if Angus tells me it means nothing.

"So, if you're not here to warn me off, what is it?"

With a cautious air, Oskar looks around the tiny shop as if he expects there to be people listening in on our conversation. Actually, there probably are people listening with all the hidden speakers and security cameras in this shopping center, though I don't expect there is anyone *actively* listening to what we are saying, although looking as furtive as Oskar is right now probably doesn't help.

"You do care about him, right?"

I nod, watching him expectantly, wondering exactly how much *he* cares about Angus, but finding I'm not jealous of that. I think Angus should have friends who care about him. Even if that's Oskar.

"He's *really* into you, so I don't know, I figure he must have said something about it."

"About what?" I frown at Oskar, perplexed. I've thought about nothing but Angus all day. I've exhausted all topics concerning him, and I have no idea what Oskar is going on about.

Oskar fixes his brown eyes on mine. "Angus told me all about the burglary." He shakes his head and looks at me pointedly as if I'm missing something. "When I said I wasn't having the greatest time sleeping on someone's floor with a fucking Doberman wandering round the house, he practically jumped at the chance of having me stay with him. Josh, you must realize he's fucking terrified in that flat. Even when I'm there, he's still fucking terrified."

"What…? What's he terrified of?"

Though of course the realization hits me like a brick glancing off my jaw as soon as I open my mouth.

I'm so fucking stupid. Angus has told me he doesn't feel safe in that flat. He's worried someone is watching him, that the burglars will return. The dark rings around his eyes and his exhaustive tiredness suddenly make so much more sense. Perhaps he's been using studying as an escape, or perhaps he's just not sleeping well at all anymore.

"Have you seen anyone, anything?" I ask, trying to keep the urgency surging through me out of my voice.

Oskar shakes his head. "He told me about his mum getting taken into the psych ward, though. I guess it's normal to be anxious after you've been through something like that, but I'm just… I'm just worried about him." He shrugs, then leans forward, his shoulders slumping.

"Thanks for telling me," I say, though I feel awful and not sure what to do.

It doesn't matter whether I think Angus's anxiety is anything to do with Eleanor's. I agree with Oskar. Angus's reaction has got to be pretty normal given what has happened. I just wish I'd listened to him more closely, perhaps even said all those stupid words I think are pointless—that it will be okay, that I would look out for him, be there. I hate to think of him worrying or scared.

I need to talk to him. To make this okay. I'm filled with the urge to do it now.

I pull my phone out of my pocket, checking the time. It's half four. Angus's exam should have finished ages ago. My heart sinks when I see there is a missed call from him forty minutes ago. I didn't hear it. I feel a bit sick as I think back to this morning, to how I needed to be on my own, not thinking that maybe Angus needed a bit of reassurance from me. About everything.

I've been so fucking selfish.

Soren chooses just that moment to appear, fixed foot scanner in hand. I mouth that I need to make a call and point to my phone before disappearing into the stockroom.

I dial Angus's number, but his phone just rings and rings. It doesn't even go to voice mail. I close my eyes and lean against the unstable wall of shoe boxes, listening to the empty tone go on and on. Eventually I put the phone down, deciding I'm going to run his battery down if I don't. He probably just can't hear it ringing. Frustrated with myself, I check my voice mail. There is a message from Angus, but when I listen, it's just garbled and cuts off after a few seconds.

Back on the shop floor, Soren is crouched in front of Oskar. From the angle I am approaching them, his position looks a little inappropriate, unless he really is measuring Oskar's feet. I clear my throat.

When I get closer, I can see he has a pen in his hand and is drawing a potentially quite explicit picture of what at first glance looks like genitalia on Oskar's mostly blank cast. I've seen Soren draw before, and although I would never tell him as much, he has a certain brash flair for it.

"Emergency?" Soren asks glancing up from his drawing. Thankfully he's not being sarcastic.

"No." I sink down onto one of the leather stools and lean forward, resting my head in my hands.

"Why are you letting him draw a penis chasing a vagina on your cast?" I mutter to Oskar.

Oskar shrugs.

Soren sits back and starts speaking in the informative, deadpan tone he reserves for saying something scandalous. "I saw it on YouTube. It's a French advert for condoms. The vagina is not interested until the penis has a condom on."

I roll my eyes.

"I am a social warrior in the battle against STDs," he carries on, smirking. "One blank cast at a time."

"What Soren actually means is that his arrogance knows no bounds," I mock whisper.

"Ouch," Soren winces. "Your words are like a knife to my heart."

"You don't have a heart."

"Only because I gave it to you, remember?"

He smiles sweetly. It has a kind of devastating effect on Oskar, which I doubt Soren is blind to, but thankfully he chooses to ignore it.

"Josh rejected me," he tells Oskar with an overexaggerated shrug, then fixes his devastating gaze back on me. "Oskar has told me all about how you crippled him, by the way."

"I'd probably be up for a repeat performance, if you're interested?" I narrow my eyes at him. "Oskar tell you it was down that stupid road I have to give you a lift to sometimes?"

"Yep." Soren frowns, concentrating on his drawing. "But you don't have to give me a lift there anymore. That part of my life is in the past."

"What? You've stopped smoking? Just like that?" I ask incredulously.

Soren's weed habit was no small thing.

And I know I'm probably being a little indiscreet with Oskar sitting there, but he must know what goes on at that house—he was knocking at the house next door the day I ran over his foot, after all.

"Not just like that. But I'm not going to bitch and moan about how hard it is. Anyway, it's for a good cause."

A good cause? I have no idea what Soren is going on about, but I don't press him further. I remind myself *I am not Soren.*

There are no more customers, and we sit on the stools talking about nothing in particular until closing time. Well, Soren and Oskar talk. I'm distracted for much of the conversation, thinking about Angus. I know Soren notices I keep checking my phone, but he doesn't say anything. As we close up, I offer Oskar a lift back to the flat, but he is meeting someone he knows in town at six, so I leave him standing by the doors of the shopping center, sheltering from the rain.

AS I drive home, the knot in my stomach just gets tighter and tighter. When I pull up outside, I know Angus isn't home yet. His flat is dark, and there is no answer when I knock. I have his spare key—its weight heavy as a river stone in my back pocket. But I don't use it. Instead I text him again as I walk slowly upstairs.

In my flat I stare at the screen of my phone and sink down into one of the kitchen chairs, feeling consumed by thoughts of him—no longer by my need to talk to him, now I just need to know he's all right.

It's nearly half six. He's not replied to any of my texts. *Where the fuck is he?*

Worry begins to unfurl its dark wings in my chest.

I'M SITTING and staring out the kitchen window when Oskar returns at eight. The world is blurred by rain—the black streets brightened by starbursts of orange streetlights that only make the darkness seem darker, the sky beyond them an unfathomable void. Someone driving a clapped-out Mini with smoke pouring out of its exhaust drops Oskar off, and he hobbles up the path to the door. Angus still hasn't returned or answered any of my texts or calls. And I've made a few.

The knock on my door a few minutes later makes me jump.

Oskar.

"Is Angus here?" he asks with a frown, shifting from foot to foot on my doorstep. "He's not home, and he's not answering my texts."

Oskar is wet and shivering, and I could easily invite him in and make him a hot drink and some toast. But I don't. I shake my head.

I need to worry alone.

Despite that, an hour later I find myself perched on the arm of the sofa with my phone in my hand looking up Soren's number. I'm not sure if I want to call him. He's just going to think I'm being ridiculous, surely, but for the first time in my life I feel like I need a friend. I need someone to interrupt my spiraling thoughts, to tell me to snap out of it, tell me that I'm worrying for nothing.

Angus is eighteen, and old enough to do as he pleases. I just have a feeling he wouldn't want either Oskar or me to worry. Plus he has no other friends nearby that I know of. I know he left me a message, but I think he would have checked his phone again by now and seen all the missed calls and the texts Oskar and I have sent him—though batteries die, phones get lost, and networks go down, so I tell myself I can't be too worried about that.

But I am worried because of how we left things. I am worried I upset him this morning. I'm worried I pushed him away too far. And

I'm worried because *he* was worried. I may be paranoid sometimes, but I'm enough of a realist not to jump to the conclusion that Angus has been kidnapped or anything. Though the thought is there, lying in wait, biding its time.

I just don't know what to think. Because for the first time, it feels my focus is wholly outside myself—I couldn't care less about *me*. What I want or feel or think or do no longer comes first. My worldview has shifted, my heading subtly altered course.

"OH MY God!" Soren answers his phone with an explosion of sound. "I've seen you use phones, but I never actually thought you'd put that skill to use to phone me!"

"Don't be a dick, Soren." I run my hand down my face. I can't seem to control the shaking any other way. My stomach is churning and I think I might throw up.

"Everything okay?" he asks, suddenly serious. Despite his tendency to gravitate toward the center of attention, he is at least perceptive.

"I'm worried about Angus." My voice won't rise to above a whisper.

"What happened?"

"Nothing, he just… he hasn't come home. His exam finished hours ago, and he's not answering his phone. Oskar hasn't heard from him either."

I wander into the kitchen and turn the lights off. I feel safer in the dark, more dreamlike, less real.

"It's 45 Conyers Road, right?" Soren says, reeling off my address.

"Yeah." I'm not sure what I'm agreeing to.

"I'll be there in twenty."

Chapter 14

SOREN DOESN'T drive—I don't know why, I've never asked—so I don't recognize the black saloon that pulls up outside. Before he gets out, I see him lean over and kiss the blonde girl driving, and I assume she must be Lucy, his girlfriend who, despite Soren's continuous invites, I've never met. Downstairs I pause outside Angus's door before letting Soren in. He's wearing the same clothes he had on at work, though his impossible energy seems a bit more controlled. Dampened, maybe.

"Hey," I say. I try to smile as I hold the door open, icy rain hitting my skin. "You didn't need to do this, you know." I'm being polite, and Soren knows it.

"You don't reach out to people much. I'd be a pretty shitty friend if I didn't turn up in your hour of need." Soren rolls his shoulders. I get the feeling he wants to hug me, but I know I'm giving off don't-touch-me vibes.

I must look like crap. I certainly feel it. If Angus walked up that path right now, I would be utterly relieved for about a minute and then completely embarrassed about my behavior for hours.

Please walk up the path right now, Angus.

UPSTAIRS, I make us both a drink of hot chocolate. Though I don't drink mine, I just grip the warm cup, feeling as though the world is spinning around too fast.

"Why in here?" Soren asks curiously, looking around.

I know he means the walls. The porn.

"I like to jack off in the kitchen, what can I say?"

I mean it to sound more wry and less depressing, but I just feel too heavy.

This was always the answer I planned to give should anyone ask. Anyone except Angus, who got the truth. *That beauty pleases me.* And these scenes are beautiful. Every one. To me anyway. The ones I wrote are just words on a page. I work in a shoe shop, and I don't have any creative flair, but the things they describe, yeah, in my head it's beautiful.

Soren leans against the table, his long caramel hair falling in his eyes as he sips his drink.

"When did you expect him back?"

"I missed his call this afternoon about half three, and he left a garbled message, but neither Oskar nor I have been able to contact him since. He's normally home when I get in from work after six. He waits in the hall for me. And he has his phone with him at all times." Especially now because of Eleanor, in case someone from the hospital rings.

I should ring the hospital, make up a lie so Eleanor doesn't worry. Or perhaps that's where he has gone. Perhaps the hospital has called with an emergency… but surely, if anything were wrong, the hospital would have rung me too. Angus made sure we were both on the contact form.

Soren looks at his watch. There is a clock on the wall behind him. It's about half nine.

"I'm being ridiculous, aren't I?" I say. A part of me wants him to laugh at me and tell me yes, of course I'm being ridiculous. The other part of me wants him to confirm that something isn't right here.

Soren shakes his head. "It's out of character, I agree."

"You think I should be worried?" I run my hands through my hair and get up, trying to take a deep breath.

"No, I didn't say that. But you seem, I don't know… is there something else? I mean, did something happen between you?"

I shake my head, then hear myself mutter, "I slept with him last night, and I didn't handle it very well this morning."

"Oh." Soren gives me an infinitely knowing look that I can't bear.

"It wasn't like that. I would never use him."

I walk over to the window and look out at the starry dark.

"So what went wrong?"

"Nothing. It was good." I cringe inside at how much of an understatement that is. It was fucking *amazing*. "But when I woke up beside him this morning, I couldn't handle it. It was too much, and I think I might have pushed him away." I turn around and close my eyes, my hands gripping onto the cold kitchen counter behind me, needing something solid to hold on to. I definitely pushed him away. "I just needed him to go. I was overwhelmed. I needed to get my head around it. It wasn't like I just chucked him out or anything. But he said he was scared that once I'd shut my door, I wasn't going to open it to him again."

"You think he might have taken what happened a bit hard?"

"I don't know. He surprises me all the time with how levelheaded he is about things, like dealing with his mum. But then Oskar came into the shop to tell me that Angus is absolutely terrified that someone is watching the flat, and he doesn't want to be there on his own."

I can't believe all these words are spilling out of me. That I'm finding words to describe the things that are worrying me. And more than that—crazily, it seems to be *helping*.

Moving toward me, Soren puts his hand on my shoulder, and I immediately shrug it off. It's one step too far.

He sighs.

"It's normal to be worried, Josh. Thousands of parents probably feel like this every night when their kids don't turn up 'til late."

"Jesus, Soren! I'm not his fucking parent, okay! And I don't want to be his fucking parent! And how is any of this normal? Nothing I'm feeling is normal!" I glare at him. "Don't look at me like that, like you know exactly what's going on in my head. You have no fucking idea."

Soren raises his eyebrow, completely unfazed by my outburst.

"You're in love with him."

My eyes go wide and I open my mouth to snap something like *You have no idea how I feel*, but the words won't come, and Soren's mouth works much faster.

"Josh, I won't believe you if you deny it. *Look at you*, for God's sake! When you love someone, you worry about them. It's normal.... It's fucking horrible, but it's completely, completely normal. I *do* know how you feel. I worry about Lucy all the time. More so now we're trying for a baby."

Shocked, I stare at him. With one sentence, Soren has managed to completely knock the wind out of me. Soren just shrugs as though he's told me he likes to go to Ikea on Sundays. And all I can think is Soren, *a father*. As I think about it, it strikes me that he'd make a pretty good one. And him laying off the weed suddenly makes complete sense.

"Might be a good idea to make a list of places he could possibly have gone," he carries on calmly. "And close your mouth," he adds, looking secretly pleased by my reaction. "It's not that shocking that I want to reproduce."

SOREN GOES downstairs to talk to Oskar and check the flat while I phone the psychiatric hospital. I ask if Eleanor's okay and if Angus has been in to see her. The duty nurse checks the visitors' book, but although Eleanor's fine this evening, Angus has not been in to see her.

It doesn't make any sense.

But if Eleanor's okay, I see no point in making up a lie as to why he's not been in, so I hang up.

When Soren returns it is with Oskar in tow. Oskar is worried too. Soren is beginning to look like he's in his element.

I phone the college to check Angus actually turned up at his exam, but the place is closed at this time of night and all I get is an answerphone message to call back in the morning.

I pace the flat, feeling better that we're doing something, but worse that Angus still isn't home. And I don't feel as willing to let my guard down around Oskar, so all my thoughts are churning around inside me.

"How about his dad's?" Oskar asks.

"Why would he go there?" I say dismissively.

After everything he told me the other day and how unhappy he seemed, I can't believe he'd want to go back there.

Soren gives me a quizzical look.

"He doesn't get on with his dad," I explain.

I don't know how much Angus has told Oskar, but that afternoon Angus took me to see his old house feels like a precious secret, and I'm not willing to share any of it with them.

"Yeah, I don't get on with my dad, but I go to see him in the nursing home every Sunday. He's still my dad," Soren says matter-of-factly. I wonder if he's just feeling the whole family thing or if that's the way things are for most people.

I DON'T really want to go and see Angus's dad, but it's the only solid place we manage to come up with. If I am going to go, I want to make the drive on my own. Soren doesn't think it's a good idea, but when have I ever listened to anyone else? He walks with me to my car. Oskar watches us from my living room window.

"Sure you don't want me to come with you?"

I shake my head. My hand is on the car door handle.

"It's going to be okay, Josh."

"Don't," I whisper. "You can't know that. No one can."

This time when Soren puts his arm around my shoulders, I don't push him away.

Chapter 15

THE RAIN turns into sleet. The half-frozen droplets smearing across the windscreen make it difficult to see. I try not to think about anything as I'm driving, but it's hard.

I'm scared Angus's disappearance is triggering something deep inside me, something I have no hope of controlling. Even more terrifying is the fact that I don't think I really care as long as I find him before it happens. Nothing is more important than him being okay. After that, the emptiness is welcome to consume me.

Dark street turns into dark street. I don't really know where I'm going. In the end I think I find the estate mostly by sheer luck rather than out of any sense of direction. After passing a few hooded, faceless figures, I remember to lock the car doors. But it's not a priority anymore.

The house that Angus told me he grew up in is imprinted on my memory even in the dark.

THE STREET is full of cars. I park in the mouth of an alleyway at the end of the row and walk. I don't anticipate this taking long. If Angus is there, he's there. If he's not….

Ghostly white light flickers through the living room curtains into the front yard. I rest my hand on the gatepost, knowing as soon as I put my foot on the path, there is no going back. The hum of television chatter floats in the air, the sound interrupted by the distant crack of cheap fireworks that don't even reach above the rooftops, though I still smell the acrid smoke they give off drifting on the breeze.

I peer in at the living room window. The eerie television light is still dancing between the shadows. The curtains don't quite join, and through the narrow gap, I can see part of a sofa with a shoeless foot hanging off it.

My fingernails dig into my palm as I make a fist and knock on the front door. The door hinges look recently lifted and inexpertly fixed back down again, the reinforced glass window smashed. I'm unsurprised when there is no answer, but still hopelessness wells up inside me—a wall of darkness I cannot surmount.

This is so hard. I'm using up all my resources just to be here right now.

It's eleven at night, and if Angus's dad doesn't know where Angus is, I don't know what I'm going to do. Angus wouldn't just vanish of his own accord. The possibility that something bad has happened to him swells sickly inside me. I hammer again on the door, louder and more persistent this time.

My first impression of Jack O'Rourke came nearly two months ago when I opened the communal door to our flats, sick of his continued hammering fist rattling the glass. I told him, in no uncertain terms, that Eleanor and Angus were not coming outside to talk to him and he could fuck right off or I'd be calling the police. He acted as if he was used to intimidating people with his presence. But I wasn't going to be intimidated—I was feeling too protective of my little nest for that. He was shorter than me and far broader, and I remember thinking his body could have been powerful if he hadn't let himself go. His stomach bulged over his belt. I'd gotten the impression he was a drinker, though I can't recollect why. The only similarity I could find between him and Angus was his unruly mass of thick dark hair.

The man with the half-empty bottle of beer in his hand who drunkenly sways as he stands in the doorway in front of me is… *diminished.* It's the only way I can describe him. Jack O'Rourke is not the man he once was. He's so much thinner—his clothes are hanging off him. His hair is a matted mess, and his face looks haggard.

"Who are you?" he asks roughly.

"A friend of Angus's."

"Fuck off." He moves to shut the door, but I shove my foot in the way.

"I'm looking for Angus."

"My son—" Jack shakes his head, and then of all things, he laughs, though there is little humor to it. "—disgusts me."

But there is no disgust in his expression, if anything, he looks upset—deeply upset—and it throws me. It makes me think that something has happened between him and Angus. Something recent.

"Is he here?" I ask, desperately wanting my hunch to be right and feeling as though my stomach is climbing up my throat.

"It's you, isn't it?" Again the warring emotions on his face—part distress, part anger. "You're the one who changed him. *Perverted* him."

What? The conversation has me lost. I'm not sure what to think.

"Get the fuck away from my house," he spits with a bit more venom this time, and he slams the door against my foot in an effort to get rid of me.

Pain lances up my leg.

I'm not angry, but I am desperate. With both hands I push the door back against him. The momentum shoves him against the wall.

"Is he here?" I repeat with a little more force as I stand over him.

"No."

"*Was* he here?"

Jack doesn't answer. It tells me all I need to know, and I'm floored by the white-hot relief rushing through me. Right now I'm not even wondering why Angus came to see his dad. I'm not even going to think about it. Finding him so I can just hold him in my arms is the only thing I want to think about.

"When? How long ago?"

Jack shrugs.

"Was he going to get the bus home?"

"*This* was supposed to be his home." He takes a long drink from the bottle in his hand. "How can *she* look after him?" he spits.

How can you? I think, stepping backwards away from Jack, away from the door, and out into the cold of the night.

IF HE'S not headed for the bus, Angus is going to be walking. Walking through this particularly unfriendly bit of South London. On his own. At night.

He'll be okay, some naive-sounding voice tells me. But I still can't trust it.

Jack O'Rourke shuts his front door, and I break into a run.

Chapter 16

THE SLEET has given way to a constant drizzle that blurs the world through my windscreen. The shadows down every street expand away from me. Even the houses are swallowed by the dark. And I'm just looking for a single solitary figure. A young man with his head down, his coat gripped tightly around him against the cold.

I drive slowly, trusting my heart to know if it sees him. *See, I am trying to trust*, I want to plead. *Just let me find him. Let me tell him I'm sorry.* I've messed this up so badly.

Not far out of the estate, I stop and text Soren to let him know what's going on.

I berate myself for not pressing Jack for more details. Like exactly when Angus left, how long he's likely to have been walking. But it's stupid to think Jack would even know.

I take a deep breath.

Angus can look after himself. He is not a kid. I need… I *have* to trust. What else can I do?

Still driving slowly, I follow the signposts and take the most direct route home. It would be pointless circling the backstreets. I don't know them like he does.

I'm on the main road when I see a figure running along the pavement ahead of me. I think it's a bit late to go out for a run, but maybe some people work so late that the night is all they have.

It's only when I've passed him that I really notice the way his dark hair is flopped messily into his face, his lean but solid build.

My heart thumps.

I hit the brakes and come to a near emergency stop in the empty bus lane.

Angus runs toward the car—a look of complete surprise on his face as he sees me get out.

"Josh," he gasps as I throw my arms around him.

He's soaked through, his face cold against my neck, his breath warm, his chest heaving from exertion. I've become so light now he is near me, the heaviness in my chest dissolving with every rapid beat of his heart.

"I was so worried about you," I whisper.

He feels so alive. I don't ever want to move again.

But I pull away to give him a bit of space, and he drops forward, his hands gripping his knees as he tries to catch his breath.

"Didn't you get… my message? Went to see… my dad. I tried… to phone you again… but my battery died."

Brushing his wet hair out of his eyes, he looks up at me as if trying to gauge my reaction.

"Your message cut off. I know you went to see him, but only because I went to see him too," I add.

"What time is it?" Slowly he stands up, his breathing becoming deeper, slower, though his chest is still heaving.

"Nearly midnight?" I guess. "I thought I was going to have to start ringing round the hospitals." I try and smile to make it into a joke, but it's not. It's really not.

"Crap. *I'm sorry*—I'm so sorry. I didn't mean to worry you." Angus looks stricken. "I knew it was late, and I had no money for the bus even. *I'm sorry*," he repeats, biting his lip, clearly upset. "You went to see my dad?" he adds, frowning, as if only just processing what I said.

"Like I said, I was a bit worried."

He holds my gaze. I feel light-headed.

As if our reactions are somehow connected, we both sink down to sit on the curb. It's freezing and wet, but my body is more aware of other things—my proximity to Angus being the main one. All my senses are on high alert, ready to respond to the slightest movement.

"How did your exam go?"

"Good." A smile flickers across his face. "You were the first person I called, you know." He nudges me with his shoulder, and I nudge him back.

"When I came out of the exam room, I felt like I had achieved something. I knew then I had to see him. I had to do it while I felt strong, I guess."

"Why?"

"I wanted to prove something to myself, to you, to Mum. I wanted to stand up to him. To just be myself and no longer feel like I'm hiding. I don't want to be that timid kid anymore. I thought if I could do that then I wouldn't be so scared of everything."

"You don't have to prove anything to me. I'm so… *proud* of you. The way you handled Eleanor going into hospital, the way you've worked so hard for this college thing. That bastard has treated you like crap, and you've shown him in a thousand ways how strong you are."

"Do you really think that?"

"Yes."

"You really hate him, don't you?" he says quietly.

"I hate the way he's treated you," I say, thinking about what Soren said back at my flat about how he still sees his dad every week even though he doesn't get on with him.

Angus's relationship with his dad is complicated. Tonight proves that if nothing else. Encouraging Angus to cut his dad out of his life would hurt him more than help him. Angus needs to come to terms with him in his own way. If that means having some sort of relationship with his dad, I have to try and support that. If it means he doesn't want his dad in his life at all, I've got to be there for him. It's not my place to do or suggest anything else.

"He's your dad, Angus. He'll always be your dad. I won't stand for him treating you badly, but I'm not going to make you feel bad for wanting to see him either. I've always got your back, whatever."

"I told him I was gay."

"Yeah, I thought you might have."

"He didn't take it so well."

I pull what I hope is a sympathetic face, though I suspect it's not too convincing when most of what I feel is this low growling anger rolling around inside me. I think instead about Eleanor giving us her blessing at the hospital. I doubt Angus being gay or straight even factors in for her. All she wants is for him to be happy and loved. And that's how it should be, isn't it?

"You're not too upset?" I ask.

Angus shrugs. "He kind of reacted how I expected." He snorts softly. "I've never told anyone else that before, you know… said it out loud like that. *I'm gay*. It felt weird. And even though my dad didn't want to hear it, it felt good to say the words." Angus looks up at me, his eyes so dark, his skin luminous in the glow of the streetlight. "You were the first person who ever said it to me. When you told me you were gay, you said it so easily, like you were telling me the sun was shining or that you liked books." He gives me a small smile. "You made me feel normal. I'd never felt normal before."

"You *are* normal."

I don't remember what I said when I told Angus I was gay. All I remember is that it surprised me that I'd wanted him to know. I remember I'd regretted it afterwards, though. Stupid me, eh?

"I'd had a crush on you for ages before that. Before you even knew me." Angus stares at his hands.

My eyes widen. I must look comical. I guess it explains the awkward weirdness we sort of got into once he knew I was gay.

"I used to get the bus past Mum's flat after school. The bus stop opposite the flat was on the route, and sometimes the bus would wait there for a few minutes at a time as people got on and paid or whatever, so then I could stare out the window and hope. I never got off, and Dad never knew. I just wanted to see Mum, and I knew he wouldn't let me. It was a few years ago when I saw you helping Mum clear out the front garden—she was giving you instructions out of the window. You were wearing these pale trousers with grass stains all over the knees, and you were smiling. You looked so kind and strong. I can't explain it, but I just knew if I spoke to you, I'd…."Angus swallows. "I'd never felt so attracted to anyone. I got the bus more and more, hoping to see you, but it was only once in a while you were there. I thought about you all the time."

"A few *years* ago…," I repeat, feeling a little shocked.

"It was a very innocent crush." He looks down. If the lights were brighter, I'm fairly certain I'd be able to see him blushing. "I used to dream of you holding me, of just lying in your arms. More than anything I wanted us to be friends, but I knew you'd see me as a kid."

For a minute we are silent. I try and assimilate what Angus has just told me, but it's hard.

"I spoke to Mum on the phone before I went to see my dad," he says quietly. "I know you gave me the money for college. You shouldn't have done that."

Oh.

Something squirms in my stomach before solidifying heavily. "I'm sorry."

I feel small and stupid. I know he must feel like I've undermined his ability to look after himself. His pride. And really, that's the last thing I want to do.

"I'm nearly nineteen. I'm not a kid," he carries on. "I want to be someone to you, not someone you have to look after. I want to be someone you can rely on. I'm going to get a job and pay you back."

I nod. Of course I understand that. "I just wanted you to have a chance. I know I didn't go about it the right way." I run my hand over my face, feeling suddenly very tired.

Angus watches me thoughtfully. I think back to earlier, how I opened up to Soren. I don't know what's stopping me opening up now.

"Oskar came into the shop today. He was worried about you. He said you're terrified of being in the flat."

Angus looks away. "I think it was my dad, or the idea of my dad, like my subconscious was telling me I can't run away anymore, that I needed to face him, to be myself and stand up to him. You'll probably think it's weird, but I think he was the shadow I kept seeing. I hope it's worked."

I do too. But that's not where I was going with my revelation.

"I don't think it's weird," I say softly. "What I want to say is, it's okay to be scared. I think everyone is of something. I'm… terrified too," I get out eventually.

Angus looks over at me curiously.

"What of?"

"Feeling like this." I pause, trying to find the right words and knowing there is only one, really.

Angus faced his fears. I'm the one being the coward by not facing up to mine.

"I'm in love with you," I say.

Angus stares at my face. I look down. The pavement glistens with freezing rain.

"It's like *whoa*." I smile, feeling uncharacteristically shy. "Like I'm so full of feeling, I'm going to burst apart at the seams."

Angus reaches out and takes my hand, grips it between his cold fingers. He looks as though he's poised to do something but is holding himself back, his breathing quickened.

I carry on speaking, needing to get my words out now I've started. "I've been in love with you for a while, but I didn't want to admit it to myself. But tonight it didn't matter anymore how fucking afraid I was—nothing else mattered. I just needed you to be okay. I know I was probably overreacting but it was as if I just couldn't help it—I'd never worried about someone so much before. And I'm sorry. I'm so sorry I've not made this easy for you. But even though I want this—and I really fucking want this," I add shakily. "There is stuff I need you to know too. Stuff that might change your mind." Angus's grip on my hand becomes painful. "But you need to be aware of it to make your choice. It wouldn't be fair otherwise."

Angus opens his mouth, and I think he's going to speak, but he doesn't. Instead he launches himself at me, and we fly back on the pavement—Angus on top of me, closing his eyes as he leans down and kisses me.

It's not all-out passion—it tastes more like relief—but it's wonderful. I wind my arms around his back and pull him down into a hug.

"Talk to me," he whispers. "Talk to me, so I can show you how much my mind is never going to be changed."

Chapter 17

WE DRIVE back to my flat. Angus locks his hand with mine the whole way. It makes changing gear a bit difficult, but it doesn't matter that we have to crawl home in second—we get there eventually. He seems to want to prove something to me still. Those words he said as we lay on the pavement are still ringing in my head. But I know I can't believe them until I have laid myself bare to him and he sees the darkness inside me for what it is. Until he knows just how broken I really am. I couldn't talk to him about that on the pavement by the side of the road, though. I think I need the safety and security of my walls around me, the thousands of words I know.

Soren is waiting on the doorstep with Oskar when we get back. He pats Angus on the back and smiles. Angus returns his smile, and though he looks a little puzzled, he doesn't say anything.

"Oskar is going to make me a famous Russian cocktail before Lucy arrives, so I'll see you at work tomorrow." Soren looks at me pointedly, and I'm grateful he's being so tactful.

After a brief moment of hesitation, I let go of Angus's hand and draw Soren into a tight hug. When I pull away, Soren is grinning widely.

"Thanks for being here," I say.

"Anytime."

Somehow I know he means it.

UPSTAIRS I want to hesitate. I want to sidestep and avoid the whole thing. I don't want to talk. Angus knows about my depression, after all, but there is so much about it that he doesn't know—how bad it gets, how bad it's been in the past.

After I close the front door, I stand blankly in the hallway. I think about boiling the kettle, taking a shower, getting changed. Anything but sitting down and talking.

Angus holds out his hand, and when I take it, he pulls me into the living room and over to the velvet sofa, flicking on the floor lamp with his foot and tugging me down to lie next to him, all squashed up and close. The patchwork quilt Eleanor made for me a few years ago is draped on the back, and he drags it over us. His shoes fall noisily to the floor as he kicks them off. He tangles his legs with mine.

It's as though we have created a little space in the world that is just our own. I know I need to let him in.

It's okay, his eyes seem to say as he strokes small circles on my side under my T-shirt, his fingers cool against my skin. It's mesmerizing. His touch is so light. I can't do anything but lock my gaze on his. And for once I desperately wish he could see inside my head, because I don't know what to say, where to start, but before I can utter a single word, Angus kisses me. His mouth completely suffuses me with warmth and heat. I can feel his smile against my lips. I want him badly. Naked. Beneath me. My desire wants to take over, but I know part of that is because I don't want to face what I have to do.

"I love you so completely," he whispers, his lips touching mine with every word. "Whatever it is, we'll deal with it together. It's not going to change anything."

How did you find me? I think, blinking back sudden, stupid tears. *How are you here with me? How have I not pushed you away with all my hang-ups?*

In the low glow of the lamp, the words on the walls look like tiny shadows. Just blurs on the old blank pages. I know them all. Some of them are my own story. They have been my life.

"I have a mental illness, Angus," I whisper. I'm aware of no other sound but that of my voice. "I tried to kill myself. Repeatedly. That's why I was sectioned. Suicide risk."

It hurts to talk about this. My gut is knotted so tight, I can barely breathe. I can feel the tears still falling. Gently Angus wipes them away.

"I hurt everyone who ever cared about me. Then I pushed them all away because I didn't want to hurt them anymore. I never wanted to hurt anyone."

"You've not pushed everyone away," he murmurs. "There's me and Mum, your friends downstairs."

"I know." I cup his face. "I know. Thank you."

I kiss him softly.

"Is this about your family?" he asks gently.

God, he reads me too well.

For a long moment we look at each other, and I think *Don't make me talk about this. I don't want to talk about this.* But this is part of it. My family is part of it. My family is the part that hurts so badly, I have to pretend it doesn't exist, or it attaches weights to my feet and drags me under.

"I don't see them anymore." I make it sound so innocuous, so unimportant. I take a deep breath.

"Because of what happened?" Angus asks cautiously.

Not everyone understands.

This is what scares me.

Even though Angus's presence is like a life raft in a stormy sea, I'm finding it hard to breathe. It's much better that I don't think too much as I speak. No emotion, just facts.

"I was fifteen when it got really bad. My parents didn't take me seriously at first. They said I was just feeling a bit down and I should get out and do stuff, try and snap out of it. Teenagers get stressed, they said—sometimes they feel a bit low. It's hormonal. It's winter.

"But I wasn't just a bit low."

I remember feeling so powerless to make them understand that I couldn't snap out of it, that I was suffocating inside.

I wrap my arms around Angus, holding him tight. He kisses my collarbone and rests his head on my shoulder. Every time he blinks, I can feel the brush of his eyelashes against my skin. I take a deep breath and carry on.

"My first suicide attempt was a few months later. I couldn't stand all the busyness—being forced to socialize, to smile, to pretend everything was okay. No one was listening to me. I felt like I was standing in the middle of a crowded room, screaming, and no one could hear me. I slit my wrists in the bath on Christmas Day. God, it made a mess. Everyone went crazy. I was kept in hospital for a few days, and I had to see a psychiatric doctor. He gave me medication—some heavy duty antidepressants that looked like yellow torpedoes and made me feel like a zombie, but I was only sixteen, and I didn't always remember to take them."

They gave me a certain *glazed-over* look. A few of the friends I had left pointed it out to me.

"My second attempt was a half a year later. It was the closest call. I overdosed on the medication, downed nearly a whole bottle of yellow torpedoes with some brandy I found in the cellar. It wasn't a cry for help that time. They pumped my stomach and kept me in hospital for much longer. I didn't know why they were keeping me in for so long at first.

"But it was because Mum and Dad didn't know what to do. I have a much younger brother and a sister, and I was tearing everyone apart. They didn't understand why I would want to end my life. Why I would do that to them—they weren't bad parents. It was as if they thought I was punishing them for something. I tried to tell them it wasn't them, but how could I explain? So I stopped talking to them. I shut down even more. Every visit just hurt too much, and I wanted them to stop coming so I wouldn't hurt them anymore. So I couldn't see it.

"When I went home, it was as if I were a stranger. The world felt so cold. I didn't want to exist within it anymore. I really couldn't take it."

I pause. I can't remember the last time I've said so many words in one go. Angus pulls back to look at me, searching my face, checking I'm okay, but remaining silent and watchful. Listening. Waiting.

"Everything got worse." I choke back a bitter laugh as I say it, because how can everything possibly be worse than what I've just described? Angus keeps watching me—his beautiful eyes must by now see to the very depths of my pathetic soul.

"After my third attempt, I spent eighteen months in a psychiatric hospital, having ECT and cognitive therapy. I was over eighteen then, so I asked to be moved somewhere a long way away. I didn't tell the hospital why, but it was so my parents couldn't visit me regularly. I can't remember much of that time. It's like a big black hole in my memory.

"When I came out of hospital, I discovered I had a bank account opened in my name. I had a lot of money and the number of the local social services, but that was all. I assumed my parents wanted to cut off all contact. An outreach worker helped me buy this flat… and then I met Eleanor. I doubt I'd be here if it wasn't for your mum." I give him a sad smile.

"Have you ever tried to contact them?"

"No… I couldn't…." *But I've missed them.* Even though my words go unsaid, I know Angus must be able to see that.

My brother and sister have grown up without a big brother to stick up for them, to give them bad advice and a shoulder to cry on. I have no idea what they think of me now. I have no idea what my parents would have told them.

There were times when I first moved into this flat when I didn't think I could take the pain of it, of how badly I had hurt everyone. When I told Eleanor I thought it was dragging me under again, she told me not to worry, that we'd get through it together. She said I was grieving, and I had to focus on getting through first the minutes, then the hours, and the days would follow on their own. She'd helped me find something to focus on—decorating this flat, the words on the pages of endless books—and most of all she believed in me.

"But since you've come to live here, you've… you've not…." Angus stumbles awkwardly over the words.

"Since that first attempt, I've felt as though I'm balancing on the edge of it. Maybe the ECT worked for me, but, Angus, depression never goes completely. It's always there in the background. Sometimes I feel as if I'm just waiting for it to call my name. And when it does… I *don't want to hurt you.*"

I brush my hand against his cheek, lean in close so our noses are touching. I love being close to him like this.

"You won't," he says.

And it just reminds me of why I held back.... He has no idea. I need him to realize.

"I can't promise that."

I close my eyes even as Angus's fingers trace along my jaw, my lips. He smells of winter air and fresh sweat. It's not unpleasant, more, it's strangely comforting. And I know he wants to comfort me. I pull him tighter in my arms. It makes me wonder if we can ever be close enough.

"When it happens it's not something I can snap out of, I wouldn't know how. It swallows me completely. And you might think I don't care, but I just *can't*. It's like I'm paralyzed inside."

Angus looks at me solemnly. "You need to tell me when you start to feel like that, so I can know."

I nod. I can try. I want to try, but....

I mirror his touch, my fingers tracing the shape of his face, his eyes, his nose.

"Sometimes my heart feels so heavy, I'm scared I can't bear the weight," I breathe. "And all there is is this great nothingness beneath me. I don't want to fall, but I know I will. Do you understand?"

"I understand." Angus holds my gaze. It hurts that he's trying so hard to mean that, to say the right things whether or not he knows at this moment what the reality entails. Perhaps it's the fact that he's trying that's important. "I don't know how you feel, I know you won't believe me if I say I do, but I can promise I will always be here for you. Always," he whispers, before pressing his mouth to mine. I shift in his embrace. God, I want to lose myself in him. Press us together so there is not a space between.

"I love you," he whispers again as if he needs to keep saying it. As if my admission earlier has given him permission. As if he knows these are the right words to say. And this time when we kiss, I'm not holding back my desire. This time when he tells me he has a condom in the back pocket of his jeans, I don't ignore him. I want to be closer than close. I want to be connected with him deeply, give myself to him in the only physical way I can.

My heart keeps unfolding like a flower opening up in the blazing light of the sun. Because I'm beginning to understand that if I fall, it will be with his arms around me, his warmth surrounding me, his words whispered in my ear. And while it may not stop my descent—nothing will—it might be the rope that I eventually learn to cling to.

WITH A tenderness bordering on awkward, we undress each other. We only get halfway done with T-shirts and belts before Angus has other ideas and gets up to unroll my socks off my feet one at a time. Curious, I prop myself up on my elbows to watch as he holds my feet in his hands, strokes my toes, and rubs his naked chest against them. I stroke my cock through my jeans, then growl as I lunge for him, ignoring his yelps and grabbing him around the waist with my legs to pull us onto the floor by the sofa with a crash.

Fitting, I think, remembering the intensity of the first time I kissed him as we lay here, half-drunk and desperate. In a heartbeat Angus moves to cover me and he crushes our lips together, his tongue hot and perfect as it explores my mouth. Still as sweet, but he's so much more confident now. Using my thumbs, I stroke down the long muscles either side of his spine, causing him to arch into me and make a sound deep in his throat. I lock my legs around his back and grind against him, careering toward completion before we've even undressed. He bites my lip and grips me so hard, his thumbs make marks on my arms when he comes. I roll him onto his back and kiss him and kiss him. The force of our coming together is bruising.

"Fuck me in the shower with the water raining down on us," he gasps, eyes closed.

I grin. I wrote that. For once I don't feel ashamed of him knowing. He knows my deepest fears—why would Angus knowing my fantasies be any more embarrassing? The impulse to share everything with him is so powerful, it consumes me.

I lift him into my arms and carry him into the bathroom.

After making sure the water runs warm and not too hot, I undress him and guide him into the shower that is fixed over my bath. He's still boneless and trembling, so I make him sit in the bathtub under the spray as I drop my trousers and climb in with him. I sink down and tenderly cup his cock and balls, lathering him up and washing him gently, playfully ignoring his advances when he tries to kiss me. His cock stiffens in my hand, and I let him go, wanting this to last a little longer.

"First time it isn't always… comfortable," I murmur, cupping the back of his head.

With his wild hair wet and slicked back out of his face, Angus looks different—fragile in a way that has nothing to do with how physically strong he may be. Even more vulnerable, perhaps.

"Please," he whispers, tugging my hand to his backside.

He watches as I roll the condom down my cock, more desire than apprehension in his expression, though the apprehension is there.

Pulling him into my lap, I take my time with him even though I want to go hard. My hand is trembling as I ease him open with one finger, then two. I watch his face for any sign of discomfort and tease him with kisses and my hand on his cock. He pants needily and reaches down to grip my hand, pushing my fingers deeper.

When I replace my fingers with the head of my cock, rubbing it against his hole in tiny circles, he drops his head back as though he's completely letting go. This is what does it for me. This surrender.

"Please," Angus begs, falling forward and running his teeth along my shoulder.

The water is warm, and I've used so much lube, everything feels so slick and so good.

With one hand on his hip, I slowly guide myself inside him, feeling him stretch around me. It's so intense, I forget to breathe.

Angus gasps, his face screwed up in pain.

And I stop.

For minutes we pause like this. Minutes where we just kiss and touch, jaws, collarbones, fingers, mouths—painful, restless minutes that seem endless until he groans and lowers himself, forcing another inch of me inside until I am buried deep.

We barely move.

"Oh fuck." Angus's expression is stunned, his eyes not leaving mine. "Oh fuck," he groans again, rocking ever so slightly, his dick in his hand.

This bare movement almost brings me over.

I want to ask what he's feeling. I want to say *Tell me*. I want to feel it too.

But all I can do is throw my head back against the tiles and grip his hips as he lifts himself and slides back down.

The noises he makes—little yelps that are such a tight mix of pleasure and pain—are fucking wonderful, whereas I can barely take enough air in to breathe and whisper his name.

I come like that, before him, so completely wiped out by the force, I can do nothing but wrap my arms around him and cling on.

"I can feel you coming inside me," he groans, ejaculating against my stomach.

Afterwards, we hold each other. The water washes over us and we don't move. I could stay like this forever. I don't want to pull out of him. We fit together so well. It's as if we were made this way.

Chapter 18

IN THE early hours of the morning, everything seems dreamlike. Our touches are sure, our knowledge of each other surer. I'm not certain if it is a dream. We've fucked as though we're tattooing a thousand desperate promises onto our skin, and now all I want is to sleep.

When I wake I find Angus propped on his side, watching me in the drifting morning light.

It's early, but not too early.

"Morning." I smile sleepily, reaching out a finger to trace his jaw. He's so beautiful, I want our time like this to be endless so I can show him how I feel and never stop.

I trace his lips slowly as though I am memorizing the shape of them and catch a flicker of anxiety in his eyes.

"We sealed the deal last night, you know," I whisper, wondering if he's worried I'll be handing him his clothes and shoving him toward the door as soon as we get up like I did last time.

Even though I'm still scared, I'm not stupid enough to throw what we have away again.

"I know," he murmurs and lies back down by my side.

Wrapping his arms around my back, he presses his head into the crook of my neck, that space reserved for lovers, for those seeking comfort or reassurance.

I can't help getting turned on by his naked proximity, especially when we are so new to each other.

I cup the base of his cock in my hand and stroke his warm inner thigh with my thumb.

"Sore?" I murmur.

"No," he whispers.

We try to draw out our pleasure, to slow it down, but it's not easy when every new exploration of skin sets you off like a rocket. We laugh. A lot. We talk a lot too. Something else I've never done so much of during sex. After that first time in the shower, I somehow lost my own inhibitions enough to ask Angus what he feels when I fuck him, when I suck him off. And he tells me, shyly at first, then cruder and dirtier the closer to orgasm he gets.

I have the day off, and we spend it in bed, on the living room floor, in the kitchen—Angus bent over the kitchen table. We christen every room and then some.

In between exploring each other's skin, we talk about tomorrow, the day after that, the future—even though I hate talking about the future—but I do it because Angus needs to. He seems to need to know this isn't some fling, a love affair that will be over by Christmas.

Early evening I light a fire in the living room, and we sit in front of it on the sofa cushions I pull onto the floor. The room flickers as it fills with warmth, and I know I have never felt so certain of what I want in my entire life.

We wear each other's clothes and eat pasta out of my mismatched bowls, our hair wet from the shower.

"What do you normally do at Christmas?" Angus asks, swirling the last of his pasta round his bowl but not eating it.

Try to ignore it like it's not happening, I think, but I don't say that.

I do a quick calculation in my head and realize Christmas is only a week away.

I get the impression Angus might quite like Christmas.

I might quite like Christmas if I get to spend it with him.

I shrug. "Nothing much."

"Can I do nothing much with you?" he asks shyly.

I smile. "We can spend it with Eleanor too, if you like. Hospitals usually lay something on, and visitors should be allowed for a big portion of the day. So we can go there. Be with her."

Angus puts down the bowl of pasta on the floor and fiddles with his leather bracelet. He swallows uncomfortably.

"What about my dad?"

I don't say anything. I don't know what to say. I wait to see what he wants to suggest. But Angus dips his head and remains silent. When he looks down like this, his hair covers his face, so I have no idea what he's thinking.

With a frown I lean over and brush his hair aside. I run my finger down his cheek.

"I've never had a Christmas without him," he whispers.

Oh.

"He misses me." Angus looks up. His eyes shimmer glassily, and I know he's trying not to get upset. "I know… I know I should probably be angry for the way he's treated me, and I am, but when I went round the other day after my exam, he looked so awful, and he was so fucking sad. He misses me. I know he does. Even though he said all that stuff to hurt me—about how no son of his could possibly be gay—I know it hurt him too."

"Come here."

I put my bowl down and pull him into my lap.

"It wasn't always bad, Josh. What I told you that day after the beach—it wasn't always like that. I don't want it to be like that." His last words come out all broken, and his shoulders tremble.

"I know." I kiss his hair. He smells of my apple shampoo, and he smells of me. Angus's childhood is not as bleak as I once feared, I know that. I know he has been loved. But the past few years have been crap for him. At a guess I'd say it coincided with his dad's drink problem getting worse.

I love you. I hold his palm open, trace the words, and fold his hand closed around them.

We're both worn out. Emotionally, physically.

We'll figure something out tomorrow, I think, though I'm not sure what.

I take him to bed and hold him in my arms until he's still and sleeping. But I don't sleep. Instead I lie awake, wondering if there is some secret way to make everything right for him. To make his dad less of a selfish bastard unable to show Angus that he's perfect just as he is, that he is so worth loving; to make Eleanor well and not so full of fear. Of course there isn't. All I can do is deal with my own fear and anxiety, and keep loving Angus as best I can, and hope that is enough. It has to be enough.

Just before I fall asleep, I come to the conclusion that perhaps it might be.

Chapter 19

FOR THE first time in my life, I buy a Christmas tree.

I buy it from the market in town at lunchtime and have to carry the stupid thing back to work. Soren laughs when he sees me half dragging, half hoisting the monstrosity over my shoulder as I walk through the shopping center and into the shoe shop, probably dropping pine needles everywhere.

"Wow, you can just about climb that thing. Size really does matter to you, eh?" he says, smirking.

"Shut up. It was the best one they had. It has a beautiful shape to it," I add a little self-consciously.

I'd made the market guy undo the netting on quite a few to see the shape of them. He hadn't been too impressed with me. This one was the least spindly, and all the branches looked evenly spread out.

"Now you're just showing off."

I store the tree at one end of the stockroom and close the door. I walk over to Soren at the cash register, wondering if I've done the right thing buying a tree. I fold my arms across my chest and pace back and forth in front of him.

"Do you think Angus will like it?"

"Does it matter? It's your flat. Your tree," Soren says offhandedly. He's reading some pregnancy magazine. The page is open on "Pregnancy, the First Signs."

"His tree," I say.

"You bought a Christmas tree for him?" Soren glances up, raising his eyebrow. "Well… does he like Christmas?"

"I guess."

I think about all the holly he's filled my flat with. Every day there seems to be more of it, hanging over picture frames and across the mantelpiece. Yesterday I found a huge spiky wreath hung on my door and long stems of ivy wound around the communal staircase. I've no idea where it all comes from, but he and Oskar spent a bit of time at the park down the road.

"He'll love it, then." Soren punches my arm, and looks at me as though I'm an idiot for worrying. "Go with it," he mouths. "Unconventional presents rock."

WHEN I get home, I'm not sure what Angus makes of the tree. He's unusually quiet as he helps me take it down off the top of my car. It's freezing, and Angus is wearing only a thin jumper and no coat, so we unfasten the tree quickly and carry it as best we can into the house. Oskar watches from the front door. I get the feeling he wants to help, so I gesture to him to follow us upstairs.

The tree is far too big for the living room, but we stick it in there anyway. I move one of my armchairs out of the corner by the window and push the tree up against the wall. The top branches hit the ceiling and bend over. I head to the kitchen for some scissors to snip them off.

Angus puts a hand on my arm before I reach the doorway.

"Leave it, Josh. It grew that way. I like it," he says quietly.

I want to ask him if he's okay, but he turns away too quickly as if he's evading anything I might say.

BOTH ANGUS and Oskar take over decorating the tree with the ten or so sets of fairy lights I bought after Soren told me I needed *something*—I couldn't just bring a tree home. Soren had taken great amusement at the fact that I had no decorations—that I'd never even *had* a tree before.

I leave them to it.

In the kitchen I can see from the explosion of kitchen utensils and pans that Angus has prepared a meal, or at least attempted to. Some sort of pie, perhaps, or a casserole. The oven is on and it smells pretty good, so I don't investigate further. Instead I hunt through the mess for the kettle and the sink and make myself a strong coffee. I need it to be strong enough to surpass the brief moment of panic I'm having at the way everything is changing so fast. Unfortunately, it's not that strong.

Does he like the tree? Does he think it's weird that I bought a tree for him? Does he even know I bought it for him? Should I make that clear? Should I just forget about it? Should I suggest he take it downstairs?

Overthinking never helps. I force myself to go back into the living room to help with the lights. When we're done, we turn off the overhead lights and switch on the overloaded socket with all the fairy lights.

"This is probably going to take out the electrics to half of South London," I say, only half joking and seriously wondering if it's going to trip the electrics in the flat. But it doesn't.

Angus has set the lights to fade gently on and off at different times, and the effect is mesmerizing. The three of us stand there gazing at the tree.

Angus takes my hand. His palm is warm, and when I bring it to my lips, all I can smell is pine needles. He leans his head against my shoulder.

"Well, I'll leave you to it.... I'll be downstairs," Oskar says, hobbling out of the room.

For the first time, it occurs to me that it might hurt him to see me and Angus together. They never really had a thing, but still, I know he likes Angus.

"Oskar, are you seeing your family on Christmas Day?" I call out.

"Yeah, my sister," Oskar calls back, opening my front door.

Oskar's sister lives in town, and I've seen her here a few times. She has two kids… they must both be under five. They stared at me once when I was coming downstairs. I pulled a funny face at them and they ran away screaming or squealing—it's hard to tell with kids. I hear Oskar playing games with them sometimes.

“You were going to invite him up here on Christmas Day, weren’t you?” Angus says as we listen to Oskar thump slowly down the stairs. He smiles.

“Only if he was going to be on his own…,” I say. Because even if seeing me and Angus together hurts, I’ve known loneliness. I’ve known how heavy its weight can be, and I’ve been crushed beneath it more than once.

“I didn’t expect you to get a tree, you know. It must have been expensive.” He stares at the tree, the lights of it reflected in his eyes like stars.

Is this what he’s worried about?

“Christmas isn’t really my thing—” I start to say.

“That’s what I mean.”

“I bought it for you. Because it’s your thing…. Are you okay?”

All at once he’s in my arms, sobbing. For a second I think I’ve upset him somehow with my stupid tree, and my heart drops, but he breathes words in my ear that sound like “Thank you,” and I hold him so tight.

“YOUR PHONE is ringing,” Angus murmurs, his arms still around me.

“I know. I’m ignoring it.”

Angus pulls away and wipes his sleeve across his eyes. Before I realize what he’s doing, he’s slipped his hand in my trouser pocket and pulled out my phone.

“Soren,” he says glancing at the screen before answering it and holding it to his ear.

“Hi,” he says. “It’s Angus….” A smile plays on his lips as he backs away across the room, still holding the phone to his ear and letting Soren talk. “Yeah, we’re free,” he says happily, while I narrow my eyes and shake my head at him.

I doubt I’m going to like whatever he is agreeing to. I have a feeling whatever he is agreeing to is going to involve some loud club or bar in town. Even though I try not to let it, dread unspools inside me.

"I'm going in the shower," I mouth, thinking of all the ways I can get out of whatever Soren is going to get Angus to agree to.

The Christmas tree glows with soft pulses of light at my back. It's nice and warm in front of the fire.

A distraction is better than an excuse any day.

I kick off my shoes and pull my jumper over my head.

I don't really get Angus's attention until I start to undo my jeans. At that point he stops looking at my face and watches my hands. I slide my jeans down my thighs, stepping out of them as though I strip like this every day. I play with the waistband of my underwear before pushing them down too.

"Okay," Angus says to Soren a little distractedly. "See you later."

He puts the phone down. Swallows. "Soren says to tell you three things."

I touch my cock. Angus glances up at my face, just quickly, and gives me an "I can't quite work out what you're doing" look before he goes back to hungrily watching my hand.

Every time he tries to step closer, I move away.

"Soren can go fuck himself," I say. I sort of mean it, but I'm smiling.

Angus is turned on. Angus is easy, so easy.

"It's a Russian bar… Soren says. Oskar has to come too—I think he's addicted to cocktails like the one Oskar made him. He said we have to get a taxi. He says if you come, he'll get Emma to cover the first part of your shift tomorrow."

Angus talks quickly as if he's not really thinking about the words, as if he's afraid he's going to forget everything.

"And if I don't?"

He shrugs, still not looking at my face. I know exactly what he is looking at. I grin.

"Does this turn you on?" I step back against the wall and arch my back, stroking my cock slowly, slowly.

Angus strips off his jumper, his T-shirt. He throws them on the floor. He undoes the buckle on his belt. The fairy lights dance on his skin. All the hollows, all the shadows.

I step forward as he's bent over pushing his trousers down, and I lick across his back, his shoulder blades, his spine. He tastes salty and earthy. He holds on to me as though he's going to fall over. I lick him again, and he groans and tackles me roughly to the floor. I lie back as he straddles my hips and tries to pin my hands above my head. He's got the strength but not the inclination to be rough. I fight him a little. Just playfully.

All at once he leans his whole weight down over me and frowns.

I stop struggling. I let his hands clasp mine and hold me in place.

"Is this.... Are you doing this to get out of going out with Soren?"

I swallow uncomfortably. What would be the point in lying?

"I like having sex with you," I say, opting for being evasive instead.

Angus looks troubled. The erection that was so obvious in his shorts a moment ago has wilted. "You really don't want to go out, do you?"

I shake my head, feeling the cracks in the boards beneath my skull. Feeling the weight of Angus's disappointment sit like stones on my chest.

"I'm sorry," I whisper, closing my eyes.

His soft hands let go their grip on my arms, and he cups my face. "Hey. I'm sorry. I'll call Soren back, tell him another time or something. Maybe if he gave us a bit of warning?"

"It's been so long," I murmur. I feel awful. Angus isn't the only one who's lost his erection.

"It's okay. I didn't think."

You shouldn't have to think, Angus.

For the first time since we've been together—really together—I feel like maybe Angus has made a mistake. But I stop that train of thought before it even gets started. Pointless. He wouldn't be here if he didn't want to be. I'm hardly forcing him. He's pursued me since, well, since before he even knew me.

"Soren has been trying to get me to go out with him and his friends or Lucy for years. He thinks I'll just pretend to forget if he gives me any warning…. I guess he was just trying another tack." I hesitate and then say, "Invite him here."

Angus studies me. I know I'll never be able to lie to him. It's a good thing, but perhaps one day it'll be what hurts him the most.

"You sure?"

"Yeah. I've got a few drinks, and Soren and whoever can bring some more. Oskar can make cocktails if Soren brings the right ingredients," I add, knowing Oskar will probably be more than up for that.

"I'll call him and then"—he leans down, all smiles and warm skin—"we can finish what we started here, yes?"

Wrapping my arm around his waist, I pull him closer. *Yes.*

LATER WE lie in bed, Angus splayed across me like a warm blanket. The real blanket has been kicked to the end of the bed. The flat is warm from people, laughter.

"I'm glad everyone came here," I say, meaning it.

I bring Angus's wrist to my lips and kiss the soft skin. He loves to be kissed there. There and at the juncture of his thighs. He lifts his head and pushes his face against mine, and we kiss lazily.

It's half one in the morning, and I am exhausted. Without looking, I reach behind me and flick off the light.

"It was fun." Angus pauses, and I know he's thinking about something. "Do you think Oskar is okay?"

"With you staying up here, you mean?"

"Yeah."

Angus has yet to return to the flat downstairs at night. Every night since I told him I was in love with him, we've slept curled around each other like cats, in a tangle of limbs and impossible angles. Maybe I should make it more official. But not at half one in the morning.

"I think he probably quite likes having your flat to himself. From what he's told me, he's never had a flat to himself before."

"Yeah. I just don't want him to think it's because of him I'm not there. I don't want him to feel unwelcome."

“I think he knows it’s not because of him you’re not there,” I say wryly.

I’m almost asleep when Angus murmurs drowsily, “You miss them. You don’t have to miss them.”

I know he means my family. I open my eyes to the dark and roll away onto my side, pretending I haven’t heard his words.

I can’t, Angus, I think.

But I have no good reason for what is stopping me anymore. Other than I’m scared. Scared that if I contact them, they’ll want nothing to do with me. They’ll tell me I left it too long or they’re better off without their fucked-up son. Perhaps Angus can see how my fear eats away at me. Perhaps he can see the bright bit of hope I want to keep burning that I still have a family, that I’ll always have a family even if we never contact one another again.

But what is the point of having a family you never see?

Perhaps he’s trying to show me that whatever happens, my family is with him, that he and Eleanor will always be part of my life if that’s what I want.

I want that more than anything.

I close my eyes and hold Angus in the dark.

Chapter 20

CHRISTMAS EVE, and Angus is sleeping on the sofa, the fire glowing in the hearth. He is worn out.

We spent this morning bringing each other off slowly—agonizingly slowly. I've never had sex anywhere near as intense. I made Angus come without touching him, without letting him touch himself even. It was the hottest thing I've ever seen.

At twelve we dressed and showered and then spent the afternoon with Eleanor. For the first time since she's been in hospital, I wish she hadn't tried to hide how sad she is. It's hard to explain, but Angus spent the afternoon trying to cheer her up when he could have spent it just being with her, no expectations, no pressure.

I wanted to say to her, *It's okay to be sad that you're in hospital and not at home. It's okay to be sad that things have turned out like this. I know you wanted your first Christmas with your son in however many years to be at home, but it can still mean something. He would understand that you feel sad. Please don't make him feel like he has to dance around cheering you up.*

But it's not something you can tell someone, really, is it? And I do understand—it's crap being in hospital. Tomorrow morning we're supposed to go and see Angus's dad. It'll go how it goes, I guess. Good, bad, we'll deal with it.

I cover Angus with Eleanor's quilt and wander back into the kitchen, staring at my phone. I know what I want to do. What I have to do. Doesn't make it any easier, though.

The number is imprinted on my brain. It was the first phone number I ever memorized, and I've never forgotten it. I'll know it for always. *Home.* Guilt flickers in my chest for thinking of anywhere other than this little flat as home. But once upon a time, my parents' house was the only home I knew.

I dial the number, and bring the phone to my ear as I lean against the sink. I stare out the window at the dark, glittering brightness of London streets. When the phone rings, I try not to hold my breath.

"Hello?" An excited, girlish voice gasps.

A thousand other voices seem to ring out in the background. It sounds like a party. I stand in my kitchen with the lights off, imagining everything all lit up and bright.

"Hello?" she says again.

I open my mouth, but I no longer know what to say.

I put the phone down and lean against the table, breathing hard.

She must be seventeen now, my sister. Rose. And that had to be her, didn't it?

I can't imagine the number is no longer theirs. My parents were never ones for change.

I open a bottle of orange brandy I bought for a dessert and pour myself half a glass. It's the only liquor I have left in the house, and God, it's disgusting, but I like the way it burns inside me.

"Okay?" Angus asks as he stands in the doorway, wrapped in the quilt, blinking blearily.

The Christmas tree is making the whole flat glow soft then bright, like a heartbeat.

I nod and down the rest of my brandy.

I told Angus my parents had never tried to contact me after I left the hospital. While that's true, it's also true that they wouldn't have been officially notified until after I had left. They wouldn't have known where I was by then.

And I never told them.

"What are you doing in the dark?" he asks gently.

I hold up my phone. "Something stupid."

"It's not stupid," he says, coming to stand in front of me. He rests his head against my shoulder. I love that he knows me well enough to work me out. Who else would I be phoning in the dark on Christmas Eve but my parents?

"I don't know what to say to them," I say, pulling him into a hug.

"Hi? How are you? I'd like to maybe come see you sometime? My boyfriend would love to meet you," he mumbles against my jumper.

I poke him gently in the ribs with my phone. "You want to do it?"

He shakes his head. "Want me to leave you alone?"

When I nod, Angus kisses my cheek, then wanders slowly back to the warmth of the living room.

I pick up the phone.

And lay it back down on the table.

I pour myself another glass of brandy. I probably should do this a little more sober, but I'm losing courage by the second.

Riding the burn of the alcohol, I hit the redial button, hold the phone to my ear, and close my eyes.

"Hello?" The girl is cautious this time when she picks up. She thinks someone is playing a joke.

"Rose?"

"Yes. Who is this?"

I can hear music in the background more clearly now. "Silent Night," my favorite Christmas carol. I can even imagine the room all decked out as it was when I was a kid, but the people are all a faceless blank. Even Rose.

I remember her at ten—her blond curls always pinned up on top of her head, her wicked sense of humor. She loved to dance and perform. She was the life of every party, whereas Toby, her twin, was quiet. Not shy, he just preferred to watch life from the wings until he was ready to join in rather than jump into the center of attention. Toby was more like me. I remember him hovering in the background at the hospital, not knowing what to say to me. The last time I saw Rose, she was angry with me. Toby was crying. I didn't feel anything then, nothing—I couldn't even get out of bed—but now I'm ashamed.

"It's Josh," I say hoarsely.

"Josh?" She pauses. "Josh who?"

I'm about to put the phone down when she shrieks, "Josh, my brother Josh?"

The moment after she says this, there is nothing but the quiet gasp of breathing—mine, hers, everyone in the room around her, perhaps. Even the music in the background has died. I hold my hand over my mouth, afraid to speak.

"What did you say, Rose?" a woman's voice asks shakily.

My mother. And even though she is nowhere near the phone, her voice reaches inside me. Her voice connects me to the past. Maybe this is a bad idea. A really bad idea. Maybe this is a trigger.

But something stops me from hanging up.

"Josh?" Rose says to me. "We don't know any other Joshes. You're my brother, right?"

"Yeah," I say softly.

"Josh?" It's my mother's voice down the phone line now, coming through the tangled network of sound waves. Even if I put the phone down, I know I'd still hear her. She sounds shocked, upset, and… I just don't know. I think she sounds so pleased to hear from me and yet so scared too. I can understand that. I feel the same.

I didn't think I'd feel like this. I didn't think it'd be so very upsetting.

I can't speak.

"Josh," she says again. "Is that you?"

"I'm sorry, Mum." They are the only words I manage to get out. Maybe they are all I need to get out.

I don't even hear Angus come into the kitchen, but suddenly he is there, kneeling in front of me. His warm, gentle hands stroke down my back in long soothing movements while I lean forward in the chair and sob.

"Josh, it's so good to hear from you," my mother gasps.

She calls for my dad to come to the phone. He says my name, and I can hear him breathing, imagine them all standing around the phone.

For a moment no one speaks.

Angus stops stroking my back and hugs me.

"Is Toby there?"

"Yes, he's here," my father answers, and there is a rumbled "Yeah" I take to be Toby's voice.

I hate that I've left calling them so long. All I've done is hurt them. The guilt is almost enough to make me put down the phone. But again, I don't.

"How are you? Where are you living?" my mother asks, her voice tight. She's trying so hard not to cry. I could always tell when she was trying to put "a brave face on things," as she'd say.

Wiping my eyes, I sit up and take a deep breath. Angus gets up and pulls the other kitchen chair over so that he can sit next to me. I stare at his bare feet, and he flexes his toes against mine. His feet are beautiful.

"I'm doing okay. I'm living in South London. We should… we should meet."

Angus squeezes my hand so tightly as I say this.

"Josh, we would love to," my mother says quickly.

Her eagerness scares me a little. I'm scared she's going to suggest we meet tomorrow or the day after or something, and it's too soon. If I've learned anything over the years (mostly from bitter experience, and not from seeing psychs and being in hospital), it's that I need time to get my head around things, prepare myself. Impulsivity like this is about the worst thing in the world for me. It's taken me so long to build up to this phone call.

"You could come here, Josh. You are always welcome here. Or if you'd rather meet somewhere else first, just tell us where, and we'll be there."

"I'd like that. Maybe in the New Year."

"Okay. Can we… can we call you sometime?"

My throat is tight. I can hardly speak. "Yes, of course."

We don't say much more. I can't. I leave my number with them, my address.

It's enough. For now it's enough.

Angus wraps his arms around me, and I rest my head on his shoulder. I'm not sure what I feel, it's a whole mixture of things, I think. None of them bad. None of them crushing. All I need is time, and for Angus to hold me until I come together.

And he does.

He always will.

Chapter 21

Six months later

"OH MY God, look! There, look, that's a foot! It's like there's an alien moving around inside her!"

Soren holds his phone out, resting it on the table in the pub so that I can watch a video of Lucy's pregnant belly undulating as the baby moves inside her.

"Don't say that to her. That's your kid in there!" Angus says, placing a tray of drinks on the table and squeezing onto the leather sofa next to me.

I like that he does this. There is a whole seat free on the other side of me, and yet he prefers to sit so close, he may as well be in my lap.

I put my arm around him, not really giving a fuck if we get stared at. It's Tuesday lunchtime, and the pub is mostly empty anyway.

"Oh, she was the one who said it to me. She thinks it's hilarious," Soren replies.

I can believe that. Soren and Lucy are made for each other.

Strangely, the whole birth thing has yet to make me squeamish. I even sat through a birthing video last week at Soren's house. Lucy jokingly asked me and Angus to be her birthing partners when Soren began to look a little green.

Angus thinks it's pain that makes me squeamish rather than just blood, and while giving birth looks agonizing, it's a positive sort of pain. There is a point to it. A beautiful reason.

Perhaps I'm envious. I don't know. I do know that Soren's kid is going to be adored.

And if Soren did bow out, I know Angus would love to be Lucy's birthing partner, and he'd be wonderful at it too. Seeing his confidence grow, especially since he started college, has made me happier than I ever imagined.

I turn my head, pressing my face into his hair. “You smell delicious,” I whisper.

Angus pushes his face into my neck, his lips brushing against my skin, his warm breath making me shiver. He turns me on so easily as if he flicks a switch in my brain with his presence.

I smile as Soren rolls his eyes. He won’t say we’re embarrassing him—he’d be more likely to say he feels left out and we should stop because watching us turns him on. He wouldn’t mean it, though. Lucy is his world.

And anyway, Soren is going back to work in a minute. He’s left Oskar in charge at the shop—his newest employee is his most hardworking, I suspect—whereas I have the afternoon off. Though what I want to do to Angus will have to wait until later. Much later.

AT ONE o’clock we leave the pub. The afternoon sky is blue and gold, its brightness overwhelming. “It’s a nice day for a drive” as my mother would say, and this afternoon we are driving two hundred miles north to see her and my father and my brother and sister and the house where I grew up. I’m trying not to think about it too much.

Angus grabs my hand and phones Eleanor. Tells her we’re on our way.

She wanted us to pop in to the hospital to see her before we left. She only has another week there now, and she’s been home every Saturday for the past month to build up her confidence.

I think she wants to reassure me everything’s going to be okay. She knows I’m worried. The last time I saw my parents’ house was from the back of an ambulance.

“I’ve got this feeling everything’s going to be okay,” Angus says after he has put the phone down.

“Eleanor tell you to say that?”

Angus squeezes my hand and smiles—he's always smiling.

We walk through town to the car park where we left Angus's nearly clapped-out powder blue Escort. It's newer than my car and so far more reliable, which is why we're taking it instead of my crappy rust bucket (which I still love).

It also has the most comfortable seats I've ever sat in.

Angus told his dad he wanted to learn to drive, and a week later this car was sat outside the flats, its key through the front door. That sort of sums up their relationship a lot of the time, but they do have a relationship. I refused to teach Angus to drive it, insisting we'd end up hating each other, so he's taking lessons. I'm insured to drive it until he can.

As we reach the car, I look around to make sure we're not being watched and gently push Angus up against the warm metal and glass of the door and brush my lips against his. He melts against me—he always does—but I don't do it again. I just hold him close. It's enough. Being with him is enough. Enough to rearrange my heart, my trust, my world.

His eyes swallow me. He brings his arm up to cup my skull and kisses me again.

"I don't care who knows this," he whispers.

Sometimes when I look at him, I think I know him so well, and at other times I know nothing. He's changing, but it's not a bad thing. His growing confidence and the quirks that come with it are like warmth inside me. Like an ever-burning flame that will only get brighter and brighter.

"You're thinking," he murmurs. "I hope you're thinking about later, like, much later."

I laugh. "I am now." I smile and open the car door for him, and he slips inside. I could watch the way he moves all day. How graceful he is in everything he does. "And we don't have to sneak around."

I wasn't sure what my parents made of Angus when we met them in January for dinner at a London restaurant—and though I probably made it pretty clear by holding his hand and kissing his cheek, I didn't explicitly state we were together. When my mum phoned last night to check everything was all right and we were still coming, she told me she'd made up the double room in the attic for us, so I think she's worked it out.

I ease myself into the driving seat and start the engine.

Angus links his fingers with mine. "Not worrying?"

"No. Not worrying." I shake my head. I'm really not.

I've spoken on the phone every week to them—all of them. My parents have listened to me and not questioned my need to take this slowly. I think they realize coming home is a big thing.

"Do you still think of it as home?" Angus asks softly.

"It's my parents' house. It's like revisiting the past, I guess." My home is the one I've made with Angus. I think he knows this. "My home is with you," I say just to make sure.

"We've got a bit of tidying up to do at home when we get back," he says, pulling a face.

"I'm not thinking about it," I say firmly.

This morning we left the flat in a complete mess. We're redecorating. The kitchen was the first room to change, but that was months ago now. After Soren pointed it out to Lucy, and they closed the door, giggling and then growing silent, I knew it had to go sooner rather than later. I dread to think that their baby was possibly conceived in my kitchen. That would just be too strange.

And it's no longer my kitchen. It's no longer my flat—it's *our* flat. Angus's chaos is my chaos, and I couldn't be more in love with it.

With him. I am so in love with him.

Words still wind around our walls, but they are new ones now, added by both of us, a mixture of whim and innocence. Some of them are poems and songs. Some of them I wrote for him. And I will keep writing them.

But gone is my map of the stars on the ceiling. I don't need it anymore. What's the point of being reminded of your insignificance? Of overwhelming yourself with it every day?

The significance is what you make for yourself. My map of stars is right beside me, smiling in the sunshine, shining out from beneath his wild dark hair.

I don't need anything bigger or brighter. I have it all right here.

SUKI FLEET grew up on a boat and as a small child spent a lot of time travelling at sea with her family. She has always wanted to be a writer. As a kid she told ghost stories to scare people, but stories about romance were the ones that inspired her to sit down and write. She doesn't think she'll ever stop writing them.

Her novel *This is Not a Love Story* won Best Gay Debut in the 2014 Rainbow Awards and is a finalist in the Lambda Awards 2015, LGBT Children's/Young Adult category.

http://sukifleet.tumblr.com/
https://www.goodreads.com/author/show/7919609.Suki_Fleet
https://www.facebook.com/suki.fleet.3?ref=tn_tnmn
http://sukifleet.wordpress.com/

Innocence

By Suki Fleet

At eighteen, Christopher is restless and longs for something he cannot name. His mother vanished when he was very small, and after spending more than ten years travelling on the rivers and canals, drifting between towns and schools with mostly only his dad and brother, Jay, for company, he is desperate to escape that claustrophobic existence.

When they return to settle in Arlow, a town they haven't been back to in over a decade, everything changes.

Malachi has given up on love. He lost his heart when he lost his innocence. Now, at twenty-nine, he just exists—getting drunk, fixing cars, and playing the music he loves.

When their paths cross one night at a gypsy camp, Christopher thinks he's found what he's been looking for, but Malachi is afraid. He's afraid their love will destroy everything Christopher has ever known. They are ghosts from each other's pasts, and if Malachi's secrets are revealed, more than just innocence will be lost in their wake.

Skeleton

By Suki Fleet

Jan has given up on love, at least the romantic kind. He loves his five-year-old son Henry more than anything.

But when Henry starts school, Jan is introduced to Matthew, a very sweet but shy young man who helps out in Henry's class. Although he tries desperately to ignore his attraction, Jan finds himself falling for Matthew—he's everything Jan needs.

But amid creepy silent phone calls and possible break-ins, things start to fall slowly apart for Jan. Matthew wants to trust Jan, but the skeleton Jan has been trying to keep buried in his closet and the guilt he feels threatens to destroy everything good in his life.

This is Not a Love Story

Love Story Universe

By Suki Fleet

When fifteen-year-old Romeo's mother leaves one day and doesn't return, he finds himself homeless and trying to survive on the streets. Mute and terrified, his silence makes him vulnerable, and one night he is beaten by a gang of other kids, only to be rescued by a boy who pledges to take care of him.

Julian is barely two years older than Romeo. A runaway from an abusive home, he has had to make some difficult choices and sells himself on the street to survive. Taking care of Romeo changes him, gives him a purpose in life, gives him hope, and he tries to be strong and keep his troubles with drugs behind him. But living as they do is slowly destroying him, and he begins to doubt he can be strong enough.

This is the story of their struggle to find a way off the streets and stay together at all costs. But when events threaten to tear them apart, it is Romeo who must find the strength within himself to help Julian (and not let their love story turn into a Shakespearean tragedy).

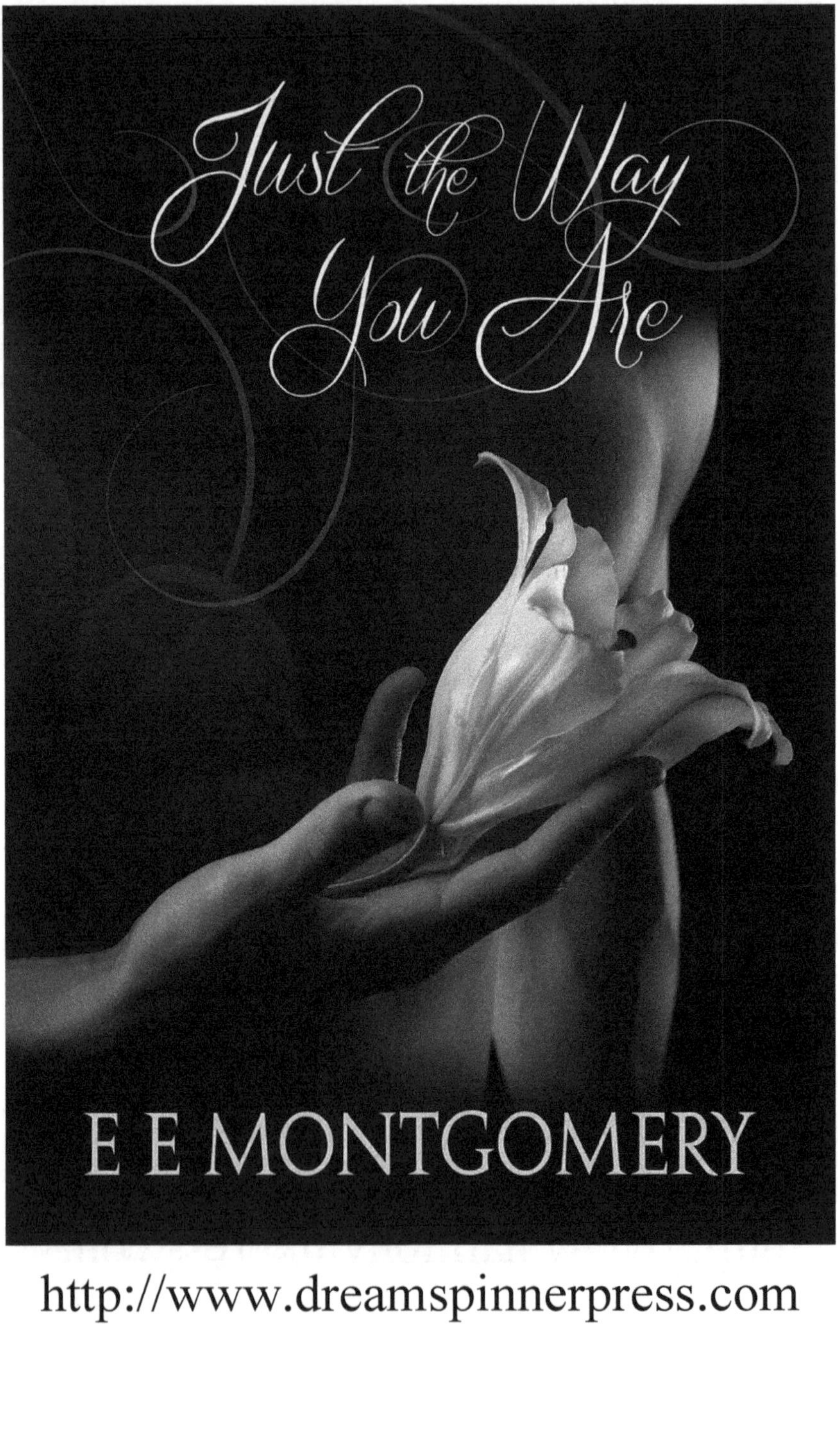

http://www.dreamspinnerpress.com

Food
FOR
THOUGHT
AMY LANE

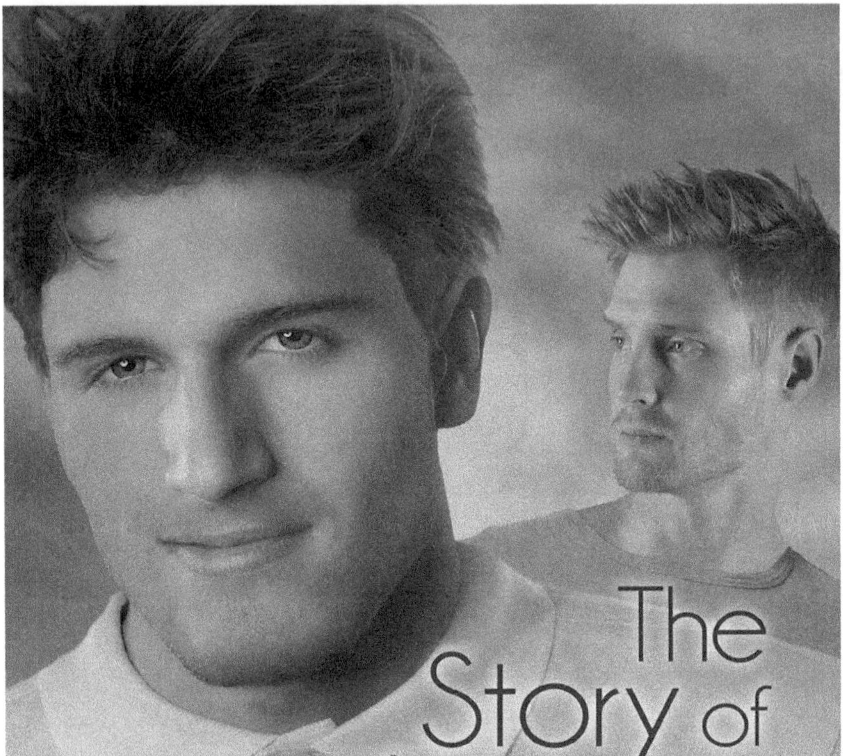
The Story of Jax and Dylan
JAMIE DEAN

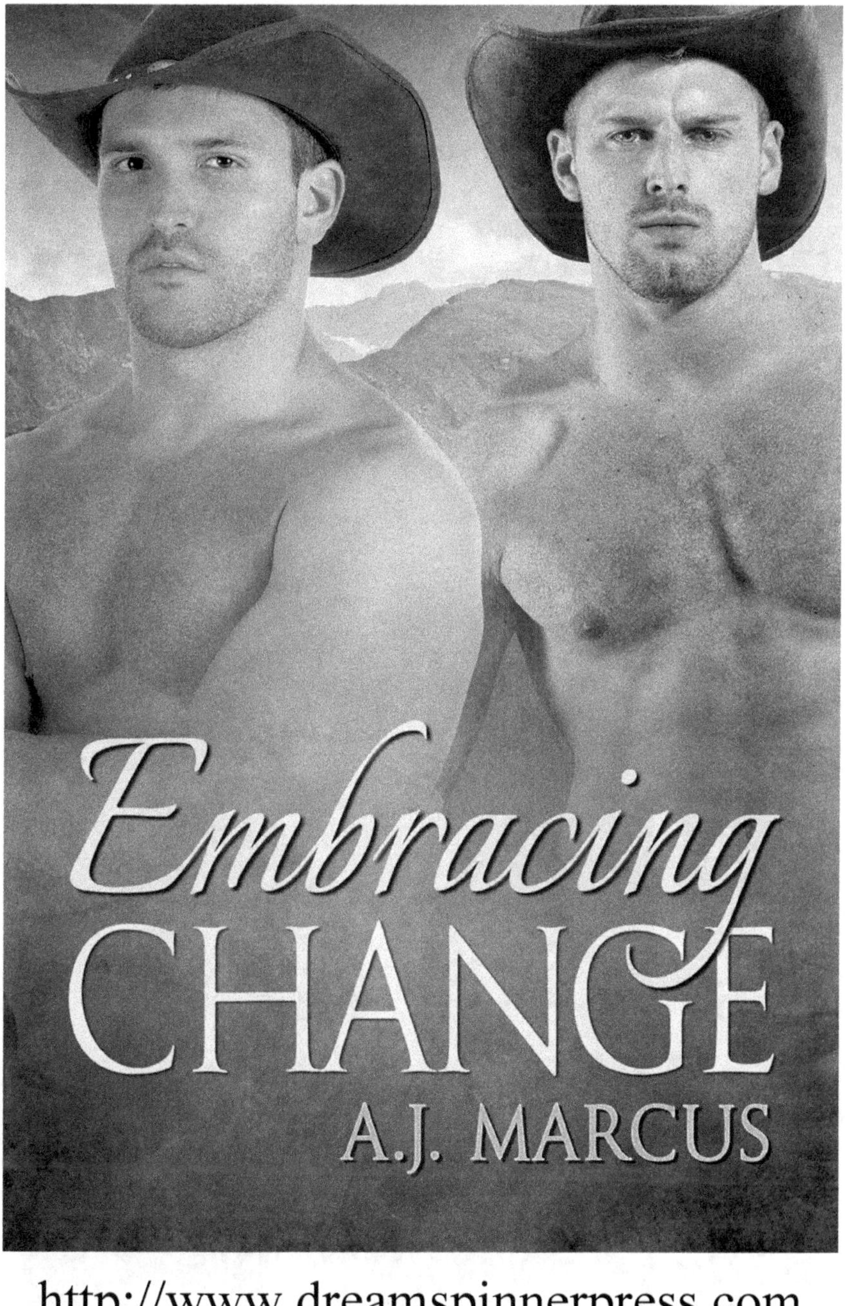
Embracing
CHANGE
A.J. MARCUS

FOR
MORE
OF THE
BEST
GAY
ROMANCE
DREAMSPINNER
PRESS
dreamspinnerpress.com

CPSIA information can be obtained
at www.ICGtesting.com
Printed in the USA
LVHW01s0001290917
550487LV00016B/1317/P

9 781634 761543